ROMANCE AT THE CAT CAFÉ

Maxine Flynn leaves behind her unfulfilling accountancy job and unsupportive fiancé to live her dream of owning a cat café. Her beloved cats keep her company, so there's no room for romance — until she meets handsome next-door grocer Angus McRae, who conceals a warm heart under a gruff exterior. But with the grocery losing money and customers, and Maxine dealing with an unwelcome visitor from her past, plus mischievous lost cats, the road to romance isn't always a smooth one. Will they be able to make a future together?

SUZANNE ROSS JONES

ROMANCE AT THE CAT CAFÉ

Complete and Unabridged

LINFORD
Leicester

First published in Great Britain in 2017

First Linford Edition
published 2020

A catalogue record for this book is available
from the British Library.

ISBN 978–1–4448–4359–0

Published by
F. A. Thorpe (Publishing)
Anstey, Leicestershire

Set by Words & Graphics Ltd.
Anstey, Leicestershire
Printed and bound in Great Britain by
T. J. International Ltd., Padstow, Cornwall

This book is printed on acid-free paper

1

The Trouble with Humans

The trouble with humans, Maxine Flynn reflected as she sized up the man on her doorstep, was that they were sometimes a necessary evil. As now, when she'd had to call in the help of this handyman-builder type person.

'I need ledges up high on the walls.' She ushered him in and waved around her newly acquired property. 'And some sort of climbing frame around the room. And some hiding places — in case someone doesn't feel like being sociable.'

Her chosen helper nodded and made notes in his scruffy looking book.

'Of course,' she carried on, 'we'll have to put a high gate across the entrance to the kitchen — I must keep a clean environment to prepare food.

And there will have to be CCTV cameras dotted around the place, so I can keep an eye on things here when I'm in the flat upstairs in the evenings.'

Ed MacKenzie didn't bat an eyelid at her long list of what some might consider odd requirements. He silently nodded and kept scribbling.

'So, will you be able to help me to get the place ready?' she asked after she finished reciting her to-do list.

'I should think so. It all sounds quite straightforward.'

'Brilliant.' Maxine smiled. So far, this was all turning out to be a lot less fuss than she'd feared. 'How soon do you think you'll be able to make a start?'

Ed's smile dimmed a touch. 'I'm pretty busy at the moment.'

Maxine had expected that — she'd contacted Ed because she'd asked around as soon as she'd moved to town and he'd been highly recommended. It stood to reason he would be in demand.

'But it's mostly outside jobs I'm

working on. If you can bear with me, I should be able to fit this in whenever the weather turns bad.'

Maxine nodded. There was still so much to do, so many things to arrange, she could afford to be generous where timescales for the alterations were concerned.

'Thanks, Ed. I'll sit tight and wait to hear from you.'

Nice man, she thought as she showed him to the door. It was a shame she'd decided cats were preferable company to people, because otherwise they might have been friends.

'Oh, I almost forgot the most important thing. I'll need a porch inside the main entrance. Nothing structural, so we won't need to involve building control, just some sort of partition with a door. We don't want anyone escaping, so we need to create some sort of double-door air-lock type situation for comings and goings.'

That did get a reaction. His eyebrows disappeared into his hairline. 'Forgive me for prying, but I have to ask. Who, exactly, are we trying to keep from escaping?'

'The cats,' she said. 'It's the cats who I'll need to keep in. I'm opening a cat café.'

★ ★ ★

'A cat café?' Angus McRae, Maxine's new neighbour and fellow business-person, rang her purchases through the till. 'What on earth's a cat café?'

Maxine smiled. 'A café where people can come to enjoy the therapeutic benefits of our feline friends while they enjoy a relaxing cup of tea.'

She smiled at Angus's startled expression. This wasn't the first time she'd encountered surprise when she'd explained her business idea. But enough people had been enthusiastic, so she knew it would be a success.

It had to be. This was her bright new future, she had no choice but to make it work.

4

'And the cats will be OK with visitors?' He began to pack Maxine's groceries into bags, a big frown on his face.

'The cats will come first,' she told Angus. 'Their welfare and happiness will be my priority.'

Angus shook his head as he handed Maxine her change. 'It doesn't seem right to me. And I don't think I like the idea of having so many cats next door. I sell food in here — it doesn't sound hygienic.'

'You won't even know they're there,' Maxine promised, picking up her bag. 'Besides, I'll be advertising all over the county to bring customers in, and they'll have to book an hourly timeslot. Think what that will mean for your shop; when my visitors arrive early for their appointments, they'll be looking for something to do and some of them, at least, will be bound to end up in here, buying snacks to pass the time.'

She could practically see the cognitive wheels turning as Angus considered that point.

'I don't know,' he said, but his tone was less certain than it had been only moments earlier. 'But I do know I don't like the thought of a cup of tea full of cat hairs.'

That, Maxine thought as she smiled sweetly and picked up her shopping, was why animals would always hold the edge over people. A cat would never be that rude.

★   ★   ★

For the first time in her life, Maxine spent her time hoping for rain. But as she opened her bedroom curtains a couple of weeks later, it was to find yet another cloudless sky.

Her new life was turning out to have a very slow start indeed.

Waiting around helplessly had never been her style — it was time to take action.

Ed had delivered some of the supplies already, so how difficult would it be to do some of the lighter work herself?

Still in her pyjamas, but raring to go, she went downstairs and made a start.

It was only after the third time the wood for the internal porch had toppled over that she picked up her phone. It didn't take her long to find the number she needed.

'I don't mean to be a pest,' she told Ed when he answered, 'but I had hoped you would have made a start by now.' She'd been so patient, really she had — and she knew Ed had warned her he would need to fit the job in when he was free — but time was moving on.

There was a sigh down the line. 'I'm sorry, Maxine. I'd hoped so, too. Look — are you going to be around later this afternoon?'

* * *

He began work as soon as he arrived. Maxine helped as much as she could, reasoning that the more she could do, the sooner the place would be ready.

But quite apart from that, working

with Ed was fun and time whizzed by.

'I feel horribly guilty for keeping you so late,' she said as she noticed the time.

'No problem. I didn't have any plans for this evening in any case. And this needs to get done. I'll work on a bit longer, if that's OK with you?'

'Won't your family mind?' As soon as the words were out she realised she shouldn't have said them. He might think she was trying to find out if he was single. And she really wasn't.

'I'm divorced,' he said. 'My daughter stays with me at weekends, but during the week she stays with her mum and my time's my own. To be honest, I'm glad to be here. I miss them both, and it can get lonely of an evening.'

Maxine knew that lonely feeling well. Not that she was about to confide that in Ed. Her new start meant she was going to be self-reliant as far as possible — emotionally, if not where practical improvements to her café were concerned.

'I still appreciate it, though, thank you.' She smiled.

'And maybe I have an ulterior motive for getting the work done.' He grinned. 'I told my daughter Chloe about your plans, and she can't wait to visit.'

'That's good to hear.' Maxine laughed. But then a thought occurred. Ed seemed around her own age — which meant, unless he'd married very young, Chloe might not be old enough. A cat café was no place for small children. 'How old is your daughter?'

'She'll be thirteen in a few weeks.'

Maxine beamed. 'That's a perfect. I'll make sure I reserve places for you both at the first session. Now, if we're going to work on, how about I make us some tea and maybe a sandwich?'

★   ★   ★

It became something of a habit for Maxine and Ed to work into the evening, and they made good progress. When Maxine again voiced guilt at keeping him so late, he shook his head.

'Don't worry. It's not as though I've a hot date planned.'

'Do you ever think you might like to meet someone?' Again, she knew she'd probably overstepped the mark, but he smiled.

'Maybe. One day. But not yet.'

She was pleased to hear it. She'd been worried Ed might get the wrong idea with the two of them working together so much. He was a nice man, and under other circumstances she might have been interested in him, but she really wasn't looking for relationship just now, either.

'What made you think of opening a cat café?' he asked as he picked up a hammer.

'I've always loved cats,' she told him. 'But it wouldn't have been fair to have had one of my own when I worked such long hours.' She would have had a dozen cats given the choice. 'My ex-fiancé called me a crazy cat lady because I loved them so much.'

10

Her smile dimmed. She'd been devastated when she'd realised he hadn't meant it as a compliment — or as a playful nickname. That had been the final straw for their relationship.

'What work did you do before you took this place over?'

'I was an accountant.' She shuddered at the memory. 'I'd have preferred to have trained as a vet, but I wanted to follow in my dad's footsteps and make him proud.'

The saddest part of it had been that she'd discovered too late that he was proud of her whatever she did. 'He realised I wasn't happy, and just before he died, he made me promise to follow my dream.'

The inheritance he'd left had granted her the freedom to leave behind a relationship that wasn't working and a job that bored her, and it had allowed her to chase a bright new future.

'If all goes to plan, I should have my first residents moving in shortly,' she told Ed, wanting to change the subject before she shared too much. 'We will be ready for them, won't we?'

'Course we will. There's not much left to do now. Just the cameras, really — and they won't take long.'

She'd thought about getting a security company in to set the CCTV up, but she was so glad Ed was happy to do it. Much better to have someone she trusted.

★   ★   ★

'Isn't it awful what happened with Ed?' Angus said the next day when Maxine popped into the shop for milk.

'What was that?' She put the milk carton into her bag and counted out her money.

'His accident,' Angus elaborated, popping the coins into the till. 'He hurt his ankle climbing down from some scaffolding at Smith's farm this morning. They had to take him to hospital to get him checked out.'

'That sounds serious. Is he OK?'

'He'll live. But he won't be able to work until his ankle's better. Not in his job.'

Poor Ed. She hadn't known him long, but she was pretty certain he wouldn't be happy with that state of affairs.

'I'll take a bunch of those flowers, too,' Maxine said, picking up some bright carnations.

The least she could do was visit Ed — and she couldn't go empty handed.

* * *

'Nobody's ever bought me flowers before,' he said from his comfy seat on the couch.

'Do you have a vase?' Of course he didn't — and Maxine ended up arranging the bouquet in an empty washed-out paint tin.

'Thank you.' He grinned.

'I thought they'd cheer you up.'

'They have.' His expression clouded. 'But I'm afraid this will put us back a bit at your place. I won't be able to climb to fix the cameras, or to put the wires through to the flat.'

Much as she'd been concerned for Ed, the thought had occurred to her, too. She bit her lip. 'I'll sort something out. You've done most of the preparatory work already — I think I can probably manage the rest myself.' She mentally crossed her fingers that would prove to be the case.

He nodded. 'Sorry. I've let you down.'

'Not on purpose.'

'No — but this couldn't have happened at a worse time. Not only am I very busy with work, but I was supposed to be taking Chloe ice skating for her birthday. That won't be happening now.'

'I'm sure she'll understand.'

'She will, but I feel we've been growing apart lately. Ice skating was something we used to do together when she was younger. I'd hoped this birthday outing might bring us closer.'

Maxine's heart went out to him. She'd been so close to her own father growing up. There had only been the two of them after they'd lost her mother. She felt for Chloe and her dad, and wished there was some way she could wave a magic wand over his ankle so he could keep his promise to his daughter. But she couldn't, so she made him a cup of tea and headed back towards home.

'The only thing left to do in the café,' she told Angus when she stopped by the shop to give him a report on Ed, 'is to install the CCTV. I only hope the instructions are easy to follow.'

★　★　★

Give her a spreadsheet or a profit and loss account and she was a whiz, but she really couldn't make head or tail of this camera. As she turned it over in her hands, there was a loud rap on the window. Glancing up, she saw a familiar dark mop of hair and the owner of that hair waving his arms to get her attention.

'What's wrong?' she asked Angus as she let him in. 'Can I do anything to help?'

'I thought *I* might be able to help *you*.' He picked up one of the cameras. 'Where do you want this?'

'I couldn't possibly let you . . . ' she started, but Angus had already picked up Ed's tools and was setting to work. 'What about your shop?' she asked faintly.

'I closed up early.'

Something of what she was feeling must have shown on her face, because he frowned.

'I used to be an electrician,' he told her, 'before I fancied a change of pace and took over the shop. I'm well qualified to do this, if that's what's worrying you.'

It hadn't been. She'd been surprised the grumpy man next door was neglecting his own business to help her, but she could hardly tell him that.

'Well it's very kind of you. Thank you.'

In Angus's capable hands, the installation didn't take long.

'There you go,' he said as they peered at the images of the café on the monitor that had been set up in the flat. 'You'll be able to keep an eye on all your cats from here now.'

Despite his disapproving tone, she was unbelievably touched he'd given up his time to help her. She could have kissed him — but she guessed he wouldn't appreciate it.

'You must let me pay for your time,' she said instead.

'Not necessary,' he told her. 'Just make sure you keep those furry demons away from my shop when they move in here and I'll be happy.'

Despite his extra-grumpy tone, Maxine sensed he was just a big softie.

'When will they be arriving?' he asked as he put the tools away.

'Hopefully sooner rather than later.' She mentally crossed her fingers. Not only did it make sense to open the café as quickly as possible now everything was ready, but she had an idea. After all Ed had done to help her, perhaps there was something she could do to help him with his daughter's birthday.

She didn't want to say anything yet, though — not until she knew she could pull it off.

* * *

It all began to fall into place with the arrival of two Bengal brothers — Alfie and Sam.

'Welcome to your new home,' she told them as she undid the latch on their cat carriers. Her two boys explored the place, ate some dinner, then fell asleep in cosy beds that Ed had built over the radiator.

They were settling in better than she could have expected.

She welcomed a British short hair named Max next. There was much careful skirting around involved with the other two, but the three were soon huddled up on the window sill, fast asleep.

By the end of the week, another five feline friends had taken up residence.

Eventually, she hoped to have around a dozen cats in her café, but eight were enough to be getting on with. And they were definitely enough for what she hoped she might be able to do to help Ed and his daughter.

She called by to see him the day before Chloe's birthday, when she was sure her cats were all settled.

'How's the ankle?'

'Sore.' He gave a little laugh. 'But I appreciate you asking.'

'I've had an idea. You know you said Chloe loves cats? Well, how about you both come to the café to celebrate her birthday? I know it's not ice skating, but it would be something you could both do together.'

'You weren't planning to open up for another couple of weeks, yet. Won't we be putting you out?'

'It's the least I can do — you've been such a good friend, working in your free time to help me. Besides, I need a trial run before I let paying customers in.'

He looked as though he was about to burst into tears.

'Thank you, Maxine. That's a great idea.'

★　★　★

'Is it OK to touch the cats?' Chloe asked, her eyes wide as her gaze darted from one cat to the next.

'Of course.' Maxine smiled. 'I'd prefer if you didn't pick them up, though — not unless they get onto the tables. Then you can lift them off or they'll eat your cake.'

Chloe giggled, and Maxine's smile widened as the birthday girl made for the box of cat toys and immediately began to interact with the kittens.

'I hope you don't mind, but I've asked Angus from next door through as well,' Maxine said, following Ed as he made his way on crutches towards a comfy sofa.

'I thought you said he wasn't a fan of your café.'

'He helped me set up the CCTV cameras.' She smiled as she heard the doorbell. It had to be Angus. 'I owe him.'

The proof Maxine needed that Angus was a secret softie appeared before her eyes within seconds. As soon as he sat down, he was mobbed by cats. And even though he bore their attention with a grumpy resignation, Maxine knew that nobody who was that attractive to animals could be a bad sort. It just wasn't possible.

She smiled across at him and was startled when he grinned back. He suddenly looked so much younger. And he was handsome when he smiled. Seriously good-looking.

Her heart fluttered.

She decided to ignore it, and knowing it wasn't seemly for a woman her age to blush, quickly turned away.

Looking around at her café, her cats, and the people who had been strangers such a short time ago, Maxine realised that she'd never been happier.

It had taken her a while to see it, but some humans, she decided, could be every bit as likeable as felines.

2

Must Love Cats

Over the following weeks, Maxine gave Angus as wide a berth as possible. She didn't want him getting the wrong idea. And she didn't want to give herself a chance to fall for him — which well she might.

She had the perfect excuse to stay away from him. Her café was now open for business, and every single day was a whirlwind of activity as curious customers visited and kept her busy.

It was as she locked up after the last of her customers one night, exactly a fortnight after her grand opening, that the phone began to ring. She very nearly let it go to the answering machine. It had been a long day, and the landline was almost exclusively used to make bookings, her friends preferring to call her mobile. But something made her rush across the café to pick up the receiver.

'Maxine's Cat Café,' she said brightly, reaching across to the computer to open up the bookings' screen. 'How can I help you?'

'I have a visitor,' a gruff voice which she immediately recognised as Angus's told her. 'Someone I think might have something to do with you.' There was a faint mew from the other end.

She frowned. 'You have a cat there?'

'It seems I do.' His tone was dry.

Maxine looked around. A quick count revealed eleven furry heads. The twelfth might well be hiding in any of the cubbyholes she'd had built in for that purpose — but another loud mew from the phone made her think otherwise.

She knew at once who was missing. 'Gladys,' she said to Angus. 'Do you have Gladys?'

'If Gladys is a very hairy black and white kitten, then yes, I very much suspect I have.'

'She's a Norwegian forest kitten,' she

told Angus. How had she escaped? Maxine always took great care that none of the cats would be able to leave the café, but it seemed she hadn't been careful enough.

The cat meowed again. 'She's loud as well as hairy,' he added.

'If you could hold on to her for two minutes, I'll pop straight round to fetch her.'

She was grateful, of course, that someone had found Gladys. But why did it have to be Angus? Not only did she want to avoid him as much as possible, but he'd warned her to keep her cats to herself.

Though it seemed her cats were oblivious to his wishes and were inexplicably attracted to him.

★ ★ ★

Angus was in the process of cashing up when Maxine arrived next door. Gladys had installed herself on the counter and was supervising the process.

She gave a loud meow as Maxine approached. 'Yes, hello to you, too,' she said as she picked the cat up. 'Angus, I'm so sorry. I can't imagine how she got out.'

He looked up from his till. 'Maybe she left with one of your customers?'

Maxine sighed. Customers were a necessary evil in her line of business. Though, to be fair, most of them were lovely. 'Perhaps,' she agreed. 'Where did you find her?'

'In the stock room. I thought she was a rat.'

Maxine was appalled, and in a protective gesture held Gladys closer. 'She doesn't look like a rat.'

Angus glanced at Gladys. 'No, maybe she doesn't.'

It was then she noticed the amused twinkle in Angus's eye — even if his face was deadly serious — and her sense of indignation dissolved.

'I'm grateful you kept her safe.' Maxine rested her cheek on the cat's head for a moment. 'I hate to think what might have happened if she hadn't ended up in here. Someone might have picked her up. Or . . . ' She gave a shudder, unable to give voice to her concern. ' . . . well, she's not used to traffic.'

'Maybe your CCTV footage will show how she got out,' he suggested.

Maxine nodded, hoping it might. 'Well I'd best be off. Thanks again.'

She smiled, but was glad when he didn't return the favour.

Once back at her place, she surveyed the footage, but there were no clues as to how Gladys had escaped. One minute she was playing happily in the café, the next there was no sign of her.

Maxine knew it was vital to avoid a repetition of Gladys's escape. She was on tentative good terms with her neighbour after a shaky start and she didn't want to jeopardise that.

A quick look around the café revealed no obvious weak points, but to be sure she phoned Ed and asked if he'd double check.

'Sorry to drag you here at this time in the evening. I know you'll have had a tiring day.' Now his ankle was back to full health, she guessed he'd be very much in demand.

'No problem.' He smiled. 'I was only looking forward to a lonely sandwich in front of the TV.'

She felt even worse now — she'd called him away before he'd even had a chance to eat his dinner.

Ed carefully checked around, just as she'd done herself only minutes before, but to no avail.

'I can only think one of the customers can't have been too careful with the doors,' he said, repeating almost exactly what Angus had said. 'Maybe you could keep a closer eye on the arrivals and departures?'

She nodded, though she didn't know how she would manage to be in two places. Typically, some customers would be paying for their teas and cakes while others would be leaving.

'There's nothing else for it,' she said.

'I'm going to have to employ a cat minder.'

Ed raised an eyebrow. She could see he wasn't familiar with the post title — she hadn't been herself until she'd watched a documentary about a cat lady of legendary resolve — but he said nothing. And that was why there were such good friends — he respected that she knew best when it came to the cat café.

'We'd better keep news of a job here from Chloe,' he said, mentioning his daughter with a smile. 'Otherwise she'll be camping out on the doorstep waiting for an interview.'

Maxine laughed. From Chloe's reaction when she'd visited the café with her father, that seemed a likely scenario.

'And I'll be delighted to employ her,' Maxine said. 'When she's a little older.'

'She's on at me to book another visit. I'll give you a ring when I know when she's staying next.'

'I'll look forward to seeing you both.' She smiled. 'Now, I was about to cook up some pasta. As you haven't had your dinner yet, why don't you join me?'

She earned a grateful smile for that.

★　★　★

'A cat minder?' Angus repeated slowly when Maxine shared her solution to curbing a certain kitten's Houdini tendencies. 'What on earth's a cat minder?'

'Someone who will help me take care of the cats,' she explained patiently. 'Similar to a childminder, but for cats.'

She saw the humour in his eyes before his face caught up. When it did, he didn't try to stop it — he threw back his head and a loud outburst of laughter invited Maxine to join in.

She resisted. 'I don't understand what's so funny,' she said, though that wasn't quite true. To anyone who wasn't familiar with the term, it must seem absurd.

She still refused to laugh, though. Angus didn't need to be encouraged.

Even if she didn't mind how the humour transformed his face and made him so handsome she couldn't quite bring herself to look away.

Despite her attempts to keep away from him, she knew that if she had been searching for romance, Angus might well have been a contender.

Even if he did have a habit of being rude about anything to do with her cat café.

★　★　★

Must love cats. That was the most important attribute for an employee at a cat café as far as Maxine was concerned. She made sure this requirement appeared in bold across the top of her advert before she printed it out and taped it in the window.

Over the next week, she received CVs from one hundred and twenty-three applicants. Sadly, most were unsuitable. Some lived too far away. Others were cat-crazy schoolchildren who wouldn't be available to work the hours Maxine would need. As she sifted through the applications, she slowly gave up hope of ever finding a satisfactory candidate.

But then she read an email from a woman named Sabrina Campbell. Sabrina had experience of working in a café in her youth, and also emphasised how much she liked cats.

When she arrived for interview, Maxine took to her at once. She sat with a cup of tea on the table beside her and a cat on her lap. 'We used to have rag dolls when I was growing up,' she said.

Maxine nodded her approval. 'So I won't need to explain that most of the time this job will be devoted to cleaning, grooming, and feeding.'

'No.' Sabrina laughed. 'That's what I expected would be involved with being a cat minder.'

That was a big point in her favour — the fact she knew the job wouldn't be all about playtime and cat cuddles.

Maxine took a sip of her tea. 'Can

you tell me a little about what you've been doing over the past few years?'

Sabrina nodded. 'I've been working from home,' she said. 'As a childminder. But my own daughter's growing older now, and we've had to . . . ' She paused, looked uncomfortable for a moment, before carrying on. 'I don't really have the space at home for childminding now. We've had to downsize recently.'

Realising this was a touchy subject and also none of her business, Maxine moved swiftly on. She made a note of Sabrina's replies to her standard questions, and realised she would be daft not to make an offer. Sabrina was knowledgeable, used to cleaning up after cats and children, she was flexible in terms of the days she could work, and she lived within walking distance. She was the ideal candidate all round.

'Oh, that's wonderful,' Sabrina said, beaming when Maxine offered her a trial shift. 'Thank you so much.'

'Can you start tomorrow?' she asked.

'I know it's short notice, but Saturday's my busy day and I'll need the help to make sure the doors are kept secure.'

'My daughter's staying with her father this weekend, so that will work in perfectly and I won't have to answer any awkward questions about where I'm going. I'd like to keep this quiet until I have the trial under my belt and we've seen how things are.'

★   ★   ★

Sabrina was as good with the customers as she was with the cats. She knew a number of the local visitors, who all seemed pleased to see her. And she made a huge fuss of those who had made a special trip from farther away.

When the two thirty arrivals trooped in, Maxine was ready with a greeting for Ed and Chloe. Ed had booked the slot the evening before, keen to surprise his daughter with a trip to her favourite café.

The two didn't notice her, however.

Instead, they looked past her to Sabrina. Chloe was smiling, but Ed's expression was frozen.

Maxine had been so confident in her choice of cat minder that this blip was totally unexpected.

'Mum,' Chloe said, going over to hug Sabrina, 'what are you doing here?'

Sabrina had turned pale. But she recovered quickly and mustered a smile for Chloe and her father. 'I didn't know you two were coming here today,' she said. 'Maxine has offered me a trial shift. I'm hoping to be her new cat minder.'

Ed had mentioned before that he still missed his wife, but it was more than that, Maxine realised. He couldn't take his eyes off her. Whatever the reason they had parted, it was obvious he was still crazily in love with Sabrina. And, judging by the furtive glances Sabrina threw his way when she thought nobody was looking, it seemed the feeling was mutual.

'I'm sorry,' she felt she had to say to

Sabrina as they closed up that evening.
'I didn't know Ed was your ex-husband,
or that Chloe was your daughter, or I'd
have warned you they were on the guest
list.'

'You weren't to know. I've started to
use my own name now since the
divorce was finalised — there's no way
you could have guessed.' She bit her lip
and managed a smile. 'I still can't
believe it's over.'

'I'm sorry.' Maxine didn't know what
else to say.

'It was all so daft. Ed was working
longer and longer hours and Chloe and
I barely saw him.' She sank onto a
handy sofa and Alfie — one of the two
Bengals — took advantage of a warm
lap. She absently tickled behind the
cat's ear. 'I know he was doing it for our
family, but we ended up as strangers. I
suggested we part, hoping a break would
let us both work out our priorities. But
it all got out of hand once solicitors
became involved.'

She sniffed, and Maxine offered her a

tissue. 'I'll get us some tea,' she said, wishing there was something she could do to help these very lovely people.

⋆ ⋆ ⋆

Once Sabrina had left, Maxine knew there was another apology she needed to make.

'I didn't realised Sabrina was your ex-wife,' she told Ed when he answered his phone. 'I'm sorry.'

He gave a short laugh. 'There's nothing to be sorry about. It's good she has a job she obviously loves. And if I'd thought about it, I should have realised she would apply for the vacancy. She's always adored cats. That's where Chloe get it from. It's genetic.'

Maxine smiled. She wasn't aware a feline adoration gene had been identified — it might well be nurture over nature — but there was no denying these things ran in families. She sighed as she remembered her own, still much missed, cat-mad mum.

'I've made her an offer of permanent work. I hope that won't make things awkward for you when you bring Chloe.'

'No, it won't.' He sighed down the line. 'To be honest, I've barely seen Sabrina since we parted. Whenever I collect Chloe or drop her off, Sabrina keeps well out of the way. It will be nice to see her when we visit the café.' There was a short silence, then he spoke again. 'She's asked me to have Chloe again next Saturday. I take it she'll be working?'

'Yes.'

'I wonder . . . ' His voice trailed off. And then, decisively, 'I wonder if you could book me and Chloe in for the first session at ten, please?'

★   ★   ★

'Not that it's any of my business . . . ' Maxine didn't like to gossip, but despite being completely opposed to the attraction she felt for him, Angus was working his way into her trust, and

38

this was the kind of thing she needed to discuss with a friend. 'But I do wonder why two such lovely people who obviously still love each other can't seem to work things out.'

'Nobody knows what goes on in a marriage.' Angus didn't seem too concerned and put Maxine's purchases through the till without even looking up.

But then he hadn't seen the look on Ed's or Sabrina's faces when they'd accidentally bumped into each other at the café. He hadn't seen the soft smile that played on Sabrina's face when she'd glanced across at her ex-husband in an unguarded moment. And he hadn't see the look of utter devotion on Ed's face as his gaze had followed Sabrina as she'd walked into the kitchen to fetch an order of tea and cakes.

'I have an idea,' she said.

Angus glanced up and raised an eyebrow. 'Are you going to tell me, or do you expect me to guess?'

'We need to do something to help.'

'We? You have to admit I'm the least

likely Cupid in town.' He grinned, and Maxine's heart skipped a beat. She wished it wouldn't do that around Angus. With one broken engagement behind her, she really wasn't interested in romance. And he had never shown the least bit of interest in her other than in a neighbourly kind of way.

More to the point, he barely tolerated her cats.

'I've decided not to book any other visitors into the café for the first session on Saturday. I need an excuse,' she said, 'to bring Chloe through here, so we can leave her parents alone to talk for an hour.'

'Gladys?' he suggested.

'Gladys,' Maxine agreed. 'Maybe Gladys could find her way to you again. And she's a lively wee soul. You'd need Chloe and me to help catch her . . . '

His gaze when he looked straight into her eyes sent a jolt of electricity zinging to her toes.

'Really?' he asked. 'You think they'll fall for it?'

'Well, do you have a better idea?'

She could see he thought her plan was daft. Not that she blamed him.

'Bring Gladys through before Sabrina arrives,' he told her, shaking his head as though recognising he was just as daft as she was.

And it was at that exact moment that she realised the attraction she felt for Angus could easily develop into something deeper. If she allowed it.

★   ★   ★

It was all systems go on Saturday morning. She'd told Sabrina to arrive shortly before ten, so she wouldn't have time before the café opened to notice Gladys wasn't with the other cats. And within minutes of Ed and Chloe arriving, Maxine's phone began to ring.

'You say Gladys is with you?' she asked loudly for the benefit of the fractured family she was trying to encourage back together. 'Thank you, Angus, I'll be there as soon as I can.

41

Chloe, would you come with me, please?' she asked. 'I may need your help. Gladys can be a bit too fast for me when she's a mind to it.'

Chloe glanced at her parents, who each gave a brief nod. Though from the look they gave Maxine, it seemed Angus had been right — they weren't fooled for a minute.

And neither was Chloe. As soon they entered the shop and she saw Gladys happily nestled in Angus's arms as he sat behind the counter, she glanced up at Maxine.

'You need my help? It looks like it.' Though she was grinning. 'How long do you think it will take for us to catch up with Gladys?'

'About an hour?' Maxine suggested.

'I'll fetch us some tea,' Angus said, taking Gladys with him. 'Stalking a cat in a stockroom can be thirsty work.'

In the end, it only took fifteen minutes before Ed came in to find them.

'I should be really cross with you,' he

told Maxine, but his grin suggested another sentiment.

Chatting to Sabrina later, it seemed they'd fallen straight into each other's arms as soon as they were alone.

'We've both been so miserable apart,' she said. 'We've got no choice but to make it work this time. And we've got you to thank for it.'

'If you need to thank anyone, thank Gladys for visiting Angus.'

'I think he has a soft spot for you,' Sabrina said, putting her cup back on its saucer.

'Do you?' She hadn't seen any evidence herself, but she liked the thought.

'Maybe you should encourage Gladys to visit him again. You never know, another romance might flourish.'

Maxine smiled. 'Maybe, one of these days, I'll do exactly that.' Maybe.

3

Christmas at the Cat Café

'I'm going to put details of the parties on the website tonight,' Maxine told Sabrina, barely able to keep the excitement from her voice as they prepared to close the café up for the day. 'And I'll print out a poster for the window while I'm at it.'

The cat minder raised a quizzical eyebrow. 'What parties would these be?'

'Christmas ones,' Maxine replied, surprised that she had to explain herself. What other kind of parties could there be at this time of year? And surely, as the mother of a teenager, Sabrina must be neck deep in preparations herself.

'You're having more than one Christmas party?'

Maxine nodded. 'We'll be hosting a week-long extravaganza here in the cat

44

café, right up to Christmas Eve. There'll be mince pies, and mulled wine, and maybe even a Santa with small gifts for everyone.'

'That will be a lot of work.'

'But it will also be terrific fun. We're going to have a brilliant time.'

Sabrina smiled. She'd been a big help to Maxine in the months since the cat café had opened. And she knew she would be able to rely on the same level of support now.

'I've ordered a CD of Christmas music,' she added. 'And decorations — they should arrive tomorrow; fairy lights, baubles, tinsel, a tree . . . The café is going to be fab.' She was even planning mistletoe, just in case any of her customers might be looking for an excuse to be romantic.

She sighed happily. In her old life as a responsible accountant, with a very serious fiancé, there had been no room for such frivolities. But now she'd started anew, she meant to enjoy every minute.

Sabrina laughed. 'I'm sure it will. But you do know what the cats are likely to do to the tree, don't you?'

Maxine's dustpan of leftover cake crumbs paused midway to the bin. 'What will they do to the tree?' In her head, the whole scenario was already perfect, but Sabrina's tone hinted at trouble.

'They'll climb up it,' Sabrina warned. 'And most likely knock the whole thing over.'

Maxine looked from one furry feline face to another. All presented the picture of innocence. She couldn't believe for a moment her little darlings would do such a thing.

'My cats are very well behaved,' she said, not really believing her own publicity. Most of them were angels, but then there was Gladys . . .

Gladys who was sitting on the counter, next to the computer, looking for all the world at her now with large eyes and a 'butter wouldn't melt' expression.

'No cat I've ever owned before has had a problem with a Christmas tree.'

She frowned even as she spoke. To be honest, the only cat she had shared her life with before the café had been too sedentary to even think of glancing at a Christmas tree, let alone climbing one.

She smiled at the memory. Tibby had been her mother's elderly moggy. That was where her love of cats had come from, she was sure. From her mother. She didn't remember much of her, but she knew her father had missed her dreadfully.

After they'd lost Tibby, he had resisted Maxine's suggestions that they get another cat. She'd suspected it was because it would remind him of the wife who had been taken from him too soon, so she hadn't pressed the issue.

'They're cats,' Sabrina said. 'And every single one that I've had has been drawn to the tree every single year. You've obviously been lucky up until now — but out of this lot . . . ' She paused and looked around at the dozen pairs of eyes who were watching the conversation intently. 'I'm sure you'll have at least one tree climber — if not twelve.'

As Sabrina closed the last of the blinds across the windows and went to fetch her coat and bag, Maxine resisted the urge to grimace. The cat café had been the realisation of a lifelong dream for her. Although the time had never been right for her to have a cat of her own, she had read every book she could lay hands on. She knew the theory of cat ownership to within an inch of its life. It seemed, however, she still had an awful lot to learn about the practicalities.

'Well, I'll just have to pick the tree up again if they do knock it down,' she said firmly.

And Sabrina gave a knowing smile as she buttoned up her coat.

After her cats, Christmas was her second favourite thing. The risk of a toppled tree would be well worth it.

'Before you go, tell me how are things with you and Ed?' She knew it was maybe overstepping the mark for a boss to ask her employee such a personal question, but she and Sabrina had become firm friends. Besides, she liked to take a little of the credit for her small part in rekindling the romance between them. Though if she was honest, a larger part of the credit was down to the couple's daughter and the man in the shop next door. Not to mention Gladys, who had been the star of that particular show.

Sabrina blushed prettily. 'It's all going very well,' she said. 'If Gladys hadn't managed to get herself lost in Angus's store cupboard next door, I hate to think where we'd be at now.' She picked the young cat up and dropped a kiss on her furry head. Gladys mewed obligingly. 'We're going out to dinner again tonight.'

'In that case, don't let me keep you,' she said, shooing Sabrina out of the door so she could go meet her ex-husband for their date.

* * *

Maxine wasn't quite so positive about her Christmas plans the next evening when she realised that, never mind the tree, cats and fairy lights simply didn't mix.

The café was shut, her supplies of Christmas sparkle awaited, and she was raring to turn her little corner of the world into a festive wonderland before she went to bed.

Gladys, on the other hand, was more concerned with setting up home in the middle of the new purchases.

'What are you doing in there?' Maxine asked as she fished the kitten out from the box of decorations and untangled her from the lights.

The bundle of fur in her hands gave a disgusted meow, outraged that she'd been evicted from her box, and Maxine struggled to keep her stern expression in place.

She looked around and met with eleven more pairs of interested eyes. No doubt, going by the innocent glances being cast in her direction, they were all plotting their own attempts at sabotage.

'I want the place to look nice,' she scolded as she popped Gladys onto the counter. 'You guys have to help me out here. We're going to have a lot of visitors over Christmas, and we have to make sure they enjoy themselves, so that they'll want to come back.'

Bookings for the festive season were already going well. No doubt the extra marketing she'd done had taken effect already — she'd billed a visit to here café as a perfect gift for any cat-mad human. And a number of people had taken her up on the suggestion.

Her cats remained the picture of good behaviour as Maxine propped the tree up and went to work with lights, tinsel, and baubles. And the result was pretty good, even if she did say so herself.

'Now,' she said, standing back to admire her handiwork. 'Let's take a nice photo to add to our website.'

She only turned her back for a second to get the camera from the drawer under the counter, but that was all it took. Instantly, there was an almighty crash and cats scattered all around her in fright while a lone bauble landed at her feet. Thank goodness it was a plastic one.

Without even looking, Maxine knew that Sabrina's prophecy had come true.

And, when she turned, a self-satisfied looking Gladys sat on the branches of the tree she'd conquered.

'I might have known it would be you.'

Before she could even start to tidy the place, a sharp rap at the window had Maxine nearly jumping out of her skin. 'Who on earth . . . ?'

Peeking behind one of the blinds, she squinted into the darkness. A familiar silhouette was standing by the door.

Despite the fact he'd just about frightened her witless, her heart fluttered — as it was always so apt to do these days, when she spotted Angus.

She let him in, and he brought the cold night air in with him.

'It's freezing out there,' she told him.

'You should have worn a coat.'

'Stop fussing. I didn't trek from the Arctic — I only popped in from next door.'

He looked around at the mess. 'What happened here?'

When she told him, he was silent for a moment, then he threw back his head and laughed. 'I suppose that's cats for you. You need to fix that tree to the wall. That would stop it toppling over.'

'I suppose I do.' She wondered how she would manage to do that.

'I'll nip next door for my hammer,' he offered, 'and I'll give you a hand with it.'

She hadn't expected that, though she didn't know why. Despite his initial reluctance when she'd first opened the café, Angus had been very helpful.

While he was looking for his tools, Maxine picked up the shiny Christmas ornaments that had dislodged in the fall and tried to straighten the tree. She didn't know how he did it, but within minutes the tree was stable.

'They'll be hard pressed to knock this down now,' he said, giving the branches a mighty shake.

'Thank you so much. That looks wonderful.' She could have kissed him. But she didn't imagine he would have appreciated it. And neither would she, if she was honest. Even if Angus was too attractive for his own good, Maxine wasn't interested in romance, she'd decided. Her priority was her café. 'Can I get you a hot chocolate, to say thank you?'

'If you insist. And do you have any carrot cake left?'

'I don't. But I have mince pies.'

When she came back from the kitchen, he was well settled. Gladys had climbed up to sit on his shoulder, Alfie was on his lap, and Sam was asleep on his feet. How was it, she wondered, that a man who'd told her quite clearly that he disliked cats was such a magnet for them?

She noticed, too, that he was very careful when he reached for his mug, so he didn't disturb his favourite fan, who was still sitting on his shoulder.

It was over their late-night snack that she thought to ask him what he was doing here at this time of night.

'I saw your light was on,' he said, 'and I thought it would be a good chance to speak to you about this poster in your window for your Christmas parties.'

'Do you want to book some tickets?'

'You must be joking.' He shook his head, killing stone dead any hopes she might have harboured that his attitude was softening to her business. 'I just wanted to say I think it's a bad idea. It will bring all sorts of undesirables into the area.'

'What do you mean undesirables?' She took a sip of her hot chocolate.

'Noisy, happy people full of festive cheer. And with you serving mulled wine, there's no telling what state they'll be leaving the place and wandering up the street in.'

Ah, so that was it. Angus wasn't happy about the idea of people going about town enjoying themselves.

'I'm only going to offer one glass of mulled wine each to the evening visitors, she explained. 'It's hardly going to be a rowdy turning out.'

'Still, I think you might have discussed it with the neighbours, first.'

Sometimes Angus reminded her of a really grumpy old man, although he couldn't be more than a year or two older than she was herself.

'I'm sorry,' she said, even though she didn't imagine her visitors would really cause a problem of the kind he was imagining. 'You're right. Of course I should have spoken to you.'

She quickly outlined her plans. 'So you see, it will just be usual numbers, and the café might stay open a little longer in the evenings, but only an hour or so. If you have any problems at all with my guests, then I'll have a rethink.'

He bit into a mince pie — his second — and seemed mollified.

'But while you're here,' she added, knowing it was a cheek, and knowing that she was pushing her luck, 'I wondered if I could ask another favour?'

'What is it?'

'Well I had hoped that Santa might pop in to deliver gifts — just for a few minutes each session. I wondered how you might feel about wearing a red suit and a beard.' He looked horrified and she sent him her sweetest smile. 'Please?'

★ ★ ★

'How in the world did you manage it?' Sabrina asked, her eyes wide with shock. 'How did you persuade the grumpiest man in town to put on a Santa outfit and give out gifts? He looks almost jolly, for goodness' sake. Angus hasn't been jolly in all the time I've known him.'

'I asked him.' Maxine put the hot chocolates she had just prepared onto the tray that already contained a plate of mince pies. 'Nicely.'

'I think he has a soft spot for you,' Sabrina said, not for the first time, as she took the tray.

Maxine shook her head. 'I think you're wrong. He's just being a good neighbour.'

'If you say so.' Sabrina was smiling as she made her way through to the café.

★   ★   ★

Christmas was going well. They had been fully booked all week, and now it was suddenly Christmas Eve.

This was the last party before she closed up for Christmas Day and Boxing Day. The atmosphere tonight was particularly festive, with Sabrina's cat-mad daughter Chloe and ex-husband, Ed — who also happened to be her new boyfriend — joining in the fun.

Angus had played his role of Santa above and beyond the call of duty. He had darted between his own shop and the café, not even stopping to change from his red suit.

Maxine had heard that a few of his customers had commented as he'd rung up their purchases dressed as Santa, but not even that had dimmed his enthusiasm.

Now he'd already closed his place for Christmas, he was sitting back, having handed out the last of the gifts, enjoying the festive atmosphere every bit as much as those who professed to love cats.

'What is it?' Chloe asked, trying to guess what was in the gift from the shape of the thing.

'You only have to wait until tomorrow to find out.' Sabrina gave her daughter a quick hug.

Maxine smiled. She'd tried to disguise the parcels' contents, but it shouldn't be too difficult for anyone to work out that they were all soft toys — cat ones, of course.

Chloe was still squeezing the parcel for clues when her father got to his feet and took her mother's hands in his.

'I don't want to spoil the fun,' Ed said, suddenly looking unsure of himself. 'But there's something I have to ask Sabrina — and I can't think of anywhere better to do it than here.'

Everyone looked on expectantly.

'Sabrina,' he said, getting down onto one knee in front of the twinkling Christmas tree — and Maxine nearly melted with the romance of it all. 'I love you. I've always loved you. I want us to be a family again — you, me, and Chloe.' All eyes were suddenly on Chloe, who, judging by her expression, had been expecting this. 'Will you please marry me? Again?'

Sabrina looked almost ready to burst into tears, but managed to sniff a reply. And all was well with the world as she and Ed kissed under the mistletoe.

'Well that was a shock,' Angus said as he helped Maxine tidy the last of the cups and plates away after everyone else had left. He'd shed his Santa jacket, hat, and beard, and was looking more like his grumpy self.

Though he didn't seem in any hurry to leave. Not that Maxine minded.

'The timing was a surprise, but the proposal wasn't. Not when they've been so happy to be back together.'

'Maybe not.' He handed her another plate to put away. 'I wondered,' he started, and Maxine's held her breath. Surely there wasn't a second proposal in the air . . .

No she was being daft. They barely knew each other.

But the way he was looking at her . . .

Her heart filled with dread. She liked him very much — too much, she sometimes thought — but she didn't want to marry him. She didn't want to marry anyone.

How on earth was she going to turn him down and still remain friends? It would make things so awkward with him living just next door.

'What did you wonder, Angus?'

'Well, I wondered . . . ' He shuffled awkwardly. ' . . . if you're not doing anything else that is, if you'd like to join me for Christmas lunch tomorrow?'

And she smiled, because that was a question she was very happy to say yes to.

4

Wedding Bells

'Do you think you'll ever get married, Maxine?' Chloe asked — earning herself a sharp intake of breath from her mother.

'You mustn't ask questions like that,' Sabrina scolded, allowing the fluff-ball she'd been grooming — a peach coloured Persian cat named Brian — to leap down to the floor. 'It's rude and intrusive and Maxine won't let you come by to wait here for me after school again if you upset her.'

Maxine looked up from the computer and laughed. She might have been disappointed in love, but she wasn't touchy enough to allow a lovely teenage girl's curiosity to ruffle her feathers. Besides, with wedding bells in the air for her mother, it was only natural that

Chloe would wonder about such things.

'It's all right,' she assured Sabrina. 'I don't mind answering.' She turned to Chloe. 'I was engaged once,' she said. 'But it didn't work out.'

'What happened?'

Maxine noticed that Sabrina was no longer telling her daughter to be quiet — rather she'd leaned forward in her seat, obviously interested in hearing the answer.

'He didn't like cats.'

Chloe and her mother both looked scandalised, as well they might. At the time it had upset Maxine a great deal, but she could look back on the experience now and realise what a lucky escape she'd had.

'You must want to meet someone else one day?' With the romantic soul of an imminent bride, Sabrina obviously wanted the whole world to share the same joy she felt at her upcoming wedding. 'You won't want to spend your entire life alone.'

'I'm happy as I am,' Maxine said,

meaning it. 'Between my cats and my friends I have all the companionship I could ever want.' She smiled. 'Besides, I have no time for a man. I aim to have the best cat café in the world and I need all my energies to concentrate on that.'

'You seem to be getting along well with Angus. I had thought . . . '

'Angus is a friend and a good neighbour,' Maxine insisted before Sabrina could say any more. 'That's all.'

Chloe nodded, seeming to understand that argument — even if her mother's glance was pitying as she shook her head at Maxine.

'We shouldn't be talking about me, not when you're getting married tomorrow,' Maxine swiftly changed the subject. A wedding was always cause for excitement and Maxine wasn't averse to being swept away by the romance of it all, even if marriage was most definitely not what she wanted for herself. 'Tell me, is everything ready? I can't believe you've arranged it so quickly.'

The couple had only been engaged a

matter of months.

'I know it might seem as though Ed and I are rushing things.' Sabrina turned her attention to gently brushing another of the café's twelve cats — this time Gladys, the resident Norwegian Forest kitten. 'But we don't see any point in wasting time organising a big party — not when we already had one of those last time.'

Marrying an ex-husband might not work for everyone, but Sabrina was positively glowing with happiness at the prospect.

'There wasn't much to do, in any case. Chloe and I have sorted out our outfits and our flowers and taken Ed's suit to be cleaned,' Sabrina continued. 'And Ed's booked the meal for afterwards.'

'Has he said where that will be?' It had all been very low-key and mysterious — invitations issued verbally, no wedding list and strict instructions for no presents. They'd been told what time to turn up at the church and to be prepared to go for a meal and that had been it.

Sabrina shook her head. 'He says we can all walk from the ceremony, so it will be somewhere here in town. He's promised something really special.'

'I'm really looking forward to it, wherever it is.' Maxine smiled. 'I've not had a day off since I opened this place.'

Instead of laughing, as Maxine had intended, Sabrina bit her lip. 'I'm sorry you'll have to close up.'

'Don't be daft. I can't think of a nicer reason to take a day off. Angus next door said he'd pop by to make sure the cats are okay. Though I'm sure they will be. They'll probably sleep though most of it.'

As though knowing she was being talked about, Gladys escaped Sabrina's clutches and jumped onto the counter, where she settled on the keyboard of the laptop Maxine was working on.

'Troublemaker,' Maxine muttered as she stroked the cat. But she didn't mean it. She was very fond of Gladys.

'Tomorrow,' she told the twelve felines once the place had closed and Sabrina and Chloe had gone home, 'we all get the day off.'

Nobody took much notice, but when she moved towards the kitchen so she could access the storeroom where their food was kept, twelve pairs of attentive feline eyes watched her every move. Gladys gave a hopeful meow.

Maxine shook her head. 'No cake today, I'm afraid.' Recently, all twelve cats had acquired a liking for cake — café guests now had to guard their plates with their lives. Luckily, the cats seemed almost as keen to get their paws on their cat-specific diet. She smiled as they jostled each other out of the way in their attempts to get to their bowls.

She was happily supervising her contented feline family's dinnertime when there was a knock at the door. She was tempted to ignore it — the café was closed after all, and a sign to that effect was prominently displayed.

She frowned. It might be Sabrina or Chloe. Or it might even be Angus from next door. She smiled at that thought.

As it turned out, it wasn't any of those three, but she was still happy to see her visitor.

'Ed.' She greeted Sabrina's groom-to-be with a smile. 'Come in.'

'I'm so sorry to bother you, but I didn't know where else to turn.' He was pale, his hair dishevelled as though he'd run his fingers through it a million times.

'Whatever's the matter?' She quickly closed the door so none of the cats could escape.

'Something awful . . . '

'Are Sabrina and Chloe all right?'

He nodded. 'They're fine. But I won't be when Sabrina finds out what's happened. I had one job for this wedding — and I couldn't even be trusted to do that.'

He looked so dejected that her heart immediately went out to him. 'Whatever arrangements have fallen through won't stop Sabrina marrying you tomorrow.'

'I'm not so sure. What bride would be happy to go through with the ceremony knowing there would be no reception for her guests afterwards?'

'Oh.' Maxine didn't quite know what to say. 'Oh,' she said again. 'I'll tell you what, I'll go and put the kettle on and then you can tell me all about it.'

As wedding problems went, no reception was pretty disastrous. Maxine knew Sabrina would be bitterly disappointed if she wasn't able to celebrate with her small group of guests after the ceremony.

'So, what happened?' she asked once they were sitting in the café with cups of tea by their side and a cat each on their laps.

'I'd booked a private room at the restaurant where I proposed the first time we got married. Then, when I phoned this evening to make sure it was all still OK, they told me the room had been double-booked.'

'That's awful. Did you tell them it was for your wedding?'

'Unfortunately, that didn't carry any weight. The other party is for the owner's grandmother's ninety-fifth birthday lunch. They have family arriving especially from abroad.'

Maxine sighed. 'How could this have happened?'

'When I booked the room, I apparently spoke to a junior member of staff who didn't pass my message along.'

'Oh, that's awful. Did they offer any suggestions?'

'They said we could have a table in the main restaurant, but that wouldn't be the same — celebrating in a room full of strangers.'

'No. No, it wouldn't.'

'So I wondered . . . ' he carried on. 'I know it's a big ask, but I really don't know what else to do . . . '

'What?' she asked cautiously.

'Well, this is where I proposed the second time. Do you think we could have our reception here, in the cat café?

I know you're not opening to the public tomorrow, and it would be perfect for our small party.'

She let his request sink in and immediately came up with a million reasons why it wouldn't work.

'I'm not really set up for making meals,' she said, casting her eye towards the tiny kitchen that was perfect for preparing coffees and teas and serving cakes, but was way too small to be much use for anything else.

'It needn't be anything fancy,' he said. 'Just sandwiches and cake . . . '

'I have to tell you, Ed, Sabrina's expecting something special. Would she be happy to have her wedding reception in the place where she works?'

'She really loves this café, you know that. And she's completely smitten by the cats. I think it would make it up to her for me messing up the arrangements for the meal if we were able to celebrate here with our closest friends and family.'

Maxine couldn't really argue with

that. Sabrina's devotion to duty was unquestionable — and Maxine knew she was very lucky to have found someone so enthusiastic to work here. Surely she could do this one thing for her conscientious assistant?

'OK,' she agreed at last. 'But you will have to be prepared to make things up to her, because this really will be very low key.'

'That's exactly how want things — low key,' he said with a grin, before drinking the last of his tea and disappearing off into the night.

★   ★   ★

As soon as Ed left, Maxine went into panic mode. She wished she'd been stronger — that she'd been able to tell Ed that no, she wasn't able to put on the reception here. But Sabrina and Ed had become good friends and had always been willing to lend her a hand — now it was only right that she help them. She only hoped she could do the occasion justice.

Mentally, she went through a list of what she would need to do to prepare before tomorrow. She needed to decorate the place in some way. The café was a nice, cosy place — and the cats made it extra special — but Maxine would need to make it look extraordinary for Sabrina's big day.

Fairy lights, she decided. She had a boxful of those from Christmas. Though she would have to go up into the attic to fetch them. She didn't fancy that in the dark, so she would leave those for the morning.

Then there was food. Ed had said sandwiches, so they would need to be made. And maybe some other savoury snacks.

She glanced at her watch. It was already late, so there was very little she could do tonight apart from make lists. But she would be up first thing in the morning, and she would need to be focused if she was going to get everything done.

*   *   *

The lights were on in the shop next
door when Maxine checked at six the
next morning. She knocked sharply. It
made sense to give Angus the business,
and maybe he could gather the food
items she needed together — that
would save her a bit of time.

She tried not to think that it would be
also be a good excuse to see her neighbour again. The attraction between herself
and Angus was a complication Maxine
refused to entertain.

It was so easy to reject all thoughts of
romance when she saw his grumpy
face. 'What's got you up and about at
this time in the morning?' he asked.
'Cats all right?'

'Yes, they're all fine — but I could do
with your help.'

He listened as she told him about the
problem, then he wrote down her order.

'It seems a lot of fuss to me.' His
frown reminded her of the day she'd
told him she was opening the cat café

74

next door. He hadn't been happy then either.

She sighed. 'It's a wedding, of course there's going to be a fuss. Can you help or not?'

'I'm sure I could manage that lot,' he said. 'I'll bring the stuff round to yours when I have it all together. I'll wait for the deliveries first, so everything's fresh.'

She grinned. Their eyes met for just a second the grumpy frown faded and he slowly smiled back.

Her breath caught.

'Thank you, Angus,' she managed at last.

* * *

She was wobbling here and there, halfway up a ladder and trying to dodge Gladys's attempts to catch the string of lights in her hand, when Angus turned up with her order in a large cardboard box. He put the delivery down safely in the kitchen, then went over to hold the ladder steady.

'What are you up to now?'

'Fairy lights,' she explained. 'I thought they'd make the place look a bit more special. I didn't realise how difficult it would be to manage. Especially when Gladys is so keen to help.'

'Do you want me to put them up?'

'No, no — it's fine, thank you.' Though really it wasn't. She was quickly running out of time. She was nowhere near getting the café looking how she wanted it. Then there was still the food to prepare and herself to get ready.

'You've got less than an hour to get yourself ready for the wedding,' he told her patiently.

'Really?' She'd been up so early this morning. Where had the time gone?

'You're never going to get everything done. You haven't even started on the food yet. And look at this place . . . '

'I know.' It would have been better if she hadn't started to hang the fairy lights at all — much better to have nothing rather than wires dangling down and lights trailing untidily along the floor.

76

'Let me help,' he urged from the bottom of the ladder.

She was the one who had promised Ed — it wasn't fair that Angus ended up doing the work. But time was running short. What option did she have if she was going to get to Sabrina's wedding both in time *and* properly dressed?

'You have your shop.'

'I'll close it for a few hours.'

'You can't do that.'

'Why not? It's my shop, I can do as I like with it.'

'But your customers . . . And you said this was all a silly fuss.'

'I've been short of customers recently,' he told her, his voice much calmer than it should be when talking about lack of business. 'And the wedding's important to Ed and Sabrina, so it's really not my place to judge.'

She glanced down at him, just as Gladys picked that moment to make her presence known. She began to climb up Angus's clothes until she was sitting on his shoulder.

'Aw.' He grimaced.

'I'd have to leave you alone with them.' There was no doubt he'd softened towards the cats recently, but Maxine still remembered his initial reaction when she'd first told him she was opening a cat café. Asking him to drop in quickly to check the cats were OK was one thing. Expecting him to spend time in here, getting things ready while they got in his way, was quite another.

He shrugged, careful not to dislodge Gladys from her perch. 'You need to stop worrying and get down off that ladder so you can get ready. I'll finish tidying the lights, and then I'll make a start on the sandwiches.'

'You know you'll need to keep the cats out of the kitchen and away from the food . . . ' Her voice trailed off as he gave her an exasperated look.

'I sometimes serve snacks next door. I have a food hygiene certificate.'

'Sorry,' she muttered, embarrassed for having made assumptions. 'Angus, are you really sure about this?'

He let go of the ladder and took her hand to help as she stepped onto the floor. 'Stop arguing — you're wasting time. Go and get ready.'

★ ★ ★

As things turned out, it was worth all Angus's efforts; the bride was enchanted by the sight that greeted her as she arrived for her reception.

'Oh, it's like a fairyland,' she declared, looking every inch a happy bride in her ivory tea-length dress.

'It does,' Maxine agreed, raising an eyebrow at Angus. Every corner of the café twinkled; the cats didn't quite know where to look. 'I didn't expect my fairy lights to go quite this far.'

'I had some spare lights in the shop,' he said, heading towards the door. 'Well, I'll leave you to the celebrations. Food's laid out on the kitchen counter. It would probably be best if everyone went in there to help themselves, rather than trying to bring everything through

79

at once.' He glanced meaningfully at the cats, before heartily shaking Ed's hand, then dropping an awkward peck on Sabrina's cheek. 'Congratulations.'

Sabrina took hold of his arm as he went to leave. 'Don't you dare leave after all you've done for us today Angus. Please stay.'

'Yes, do,' Ed added. 'Maxine told us how you've helped out.'

Angus glanced across at Maxine. She smiled encouragingly. 'OK,' he said. 'Thank you.'

So he joined the small wedding party that sat in the café, laughing and joking and fending off cats as they ate.

'This is the best wedding ever,' Sabrina said. 'Thank you so much, Ed, for thinking of the café for our reception. And thank you to Maxine for allowing it to happen, and to Angus for helping.'

That was as formal as the speeches got before Chloe went and turned the sound system on then they all quickly pushed the tables and chairs back against the walls. The teenager surveyed the scene with a contented smile as her parents began to dance — with infinite care to avoid treading on paws.

Maxine sat contentedly next to Angus. Gladys had made her way onto his lap and was eyeing the slice of chocolate wedding cake on the plate in his hand. Tentatively, she reached out a possessive paw. If the kitten could talk, Maxine fancied she would have cried 'mine' as it landed on the cake.

'Oh not you don't.' Maxine quickly scooped the cat up and placed her on the floor. 'Let me get you more cake, Angus.'

She reached for his plate, but instead of passing it over, he reached out and took hold of her hand. Their eyes met and suddenly, as far as Maxine was concerned, they were the only two people in the café.

'Would you dance with me?' he asked, not taking his eyes from hers.

'I didn't think you'd be the dancing kind.'

'I'm full of surprises.'

81

Chloe materialised from somewhere and took his plate away and he and Maxine both got to their feet.

It had been a long time since Maxine had danced, but as Angus's arms slipped around her, she'd never been happier.

Maybe Sabrina had been right, she acknowledged. Perhaps — one day — Angus might be the man who would tempt her to give romance another chance.

5

Lucky Number Thirteen

Maxine pulled her dressing gown tight about her as she made her way downstairs and tip-toed her way thought the café, trying not to disturb twelve sleepy felines.

Before she could reach the door, the knocking started again. Whoever was there at half past eleven at night was desperate to speak to her.

'OK,' she whispered furiously. 'Give me a chance.'

Being careful not to let any of the cats escaped through the storm porch, she pulled open the front door and peered out into the darkness.

'Angus.' What was he doing here at this time of night? 'Come in out of the cold.' He wasn't dressed for a cold evening outdoors and must have been chilly in his T-shirt and jeans.

'Sorry, I know it's late, but I saw your light was still on.'

'I was reading.' Well, if she was honest, she'd fallen asleep with her book on her face, but he didn't need to know that. 'Is there anything the matter?'

It was only then she noticed the small bedraggled bundle he was holding. 'Who do you have there?'

A pair of heart-melting kitten eyes looked up at her from Angus's arms.

'I didn't know what to do,' he said with uncharacteristic uncertainty. 'But I knew you'd know.'

In the months since she'd moved here and opened her cat café, Angus had always been more than capable and sure of himself, and her heart softened at this admission of lack of knowledge. But then he'd never pretended to know anything about cats.

She glanced around at her own café cats, who were regarding the scene lazily from their beds. Happy that none seemed distressed by these late-night visitors, she reached out and took the tiny grey tabby from Angus. She was rewarded with a half-hearted mew.

'Hello to you, too.' She cuddled the kitten close, doing her best to warm the animal. 'Where did you find her?'

'On my doorstep, would you believe? I heard a noise and went to investigate, and there she was.' He looked around, and Maxine noted that her cats all seemed to be hanging on his every word. Taking his scrutiny as invitation. Gladys took one leap and landed on his shoulder with a loud meow. 'You know about cats. Why do they make a beeline for me?'

She smiled. 'They sense a kindred spirit, I suppose.'

'What do you mean?'

'Well, cats are independent and not fond of fuss ... Remind you of anyone?'

He grinned as their eyes met — and Maxine's heart fluttered as their gaze held for just a moment longer than necessary.

'I'd better have a look at this little one. She's in a bit of a state. She must have come from somewhere. Do you think she's wandered off from her home?'

He shrugged a broad shoulder. 'You're the cat expert. But looking at her, I'd say she's maybe a stray.'

Maxine wasn't convinced. She had to have a mother somewhere. Or perhaps more likely she'd moved to a forever home and escaped. Her human family could be looking for her.

'Put the kettle on,' she told him. 'And make us both a cuppa while I see if this little one will take some food and drink.' There would be time enough to check the town's social media pages to see if anyone had posted that they were missing a kitten after she'd administered emergency care.

The kitten was cold and could do with a bit of a clean. She was evidently hungry, too — she demolished the food that Maxine offered her in a flash.

'What will you do with her?' Angus asked as he put a mug of hot chocolate next to Maxine.

Gladys took the chance to climb onto his shoulder again, after his visit to the kitchen. Maxine noticed that he seemed to be in no hurry to put her down and she suppressed a smile. Angus was gruff and pretended he had no time for the cats, but all her cats seemed to like him — and Gladys seemed to have forged a special bond with him.

'I'll check online to see if anyone's missing her. If there's nothing there, she can stay here for tonight, though I'll take her up to the flat rather than leave her here with this lot.' Twelve pairs of eyes looked at her, the picture of innocent curiosity. 'She won't be used to them, and they won't be used to her, so that's safest, I think.'

He gave a nod.

'Then in the morning I'll take her to the vet to have her checked over. Hopefully she's chipped and we can return her to her family.'

'And if she isn't chipped?'

'She might not be. She's very small,

still. In that case it will be time for posters and spreading the word to see if we can find out where she belongs. And if that doesn't work, the re-homing centre might be able to help.'

Angus didn't look too pleased with that idea. And Maxine couldn't say she blamed him.

She saw him out, holding tightly onto the new kitten as she opened the door.

'Thank you for bringing her to me, Angus.'

He paused on the doorstep, again looking uncharacteristically uncertain. 'You were the first person I thought of, Maxine.'

She smiled.

He was the first person she always thought of, too, but she didn't know how he would react if she confided that particular secret.

★   ★   ★

Maxine waited until Sabrina turned up for work the next day before she popped the little stranger cat into a cat carrier and headed off in her car.

The vet was kind and gentle, and the cat was sweetness personified as she was checked over. 'Maybe she could give Gladys some lessons in how to be a good cat,' the vet joked, referring to the last time she had encountered the most spirited member of Maxine's feline family.

'Ah, yes — I'm still really sorry about that.'

In an effort to forget the loud objections Gladys had made during her last visit here, Maxine fixed her sheepish gaze to the little cat on the table. Such a sweet cat. But Gladys was sweet, too, in her own way.

'No worries,' the vet laughed. 'Believe me, we've had much more badly behaved pets visiting us here. Some of them actively hate me — you'd never know I was treating them for their own good.'

★ ★ ★

Angus would want to hear the news, she was sure, and once she'd taken the kitten up to her flat, she popped next door to his shop.

'What was the verdict from the vet?' Angus called out as she walked through the door.

For once, the place was busy, and Maxine was aware of an interested audience of shoppers as she walked over to the counter, where he was standing.

'She's healthy enough, thankfully, but not chipped,' she told him. 'The vet thought you might be right — she could be a stray. But we should probably ask around and try to see if anyone's lost her.'

'So, posters?' Angus asked.

'Posters,' she confirmed, trying to ignore the picture of two large eyes that would keep invading her thoughts. 'And I'll post up a photo online to say she's been found.'

That would be best. There was a chance someone might be missing her, and Maxine, loving her cats as she did, couldn't imagine the pain a missing kitten would bring to her family. She sniffed as she imagined herself in their place. They would be wondering where she was, how she was, if they would ever see her again . . .

Angus gave her an awkward glance, but said nothing. 'What will you do with her in the meantime?'

Despite being emotional over the lost kitten's family, she was on the verge of teasing him by suggesting the kitten could stay with him. She would love to see how he might cope with the suggestion. That wouldn't be fair, though, not when he'd gone to so much trouble for this one.

'She can stay with me in the flat,' she decided, though when she saw the expression of relief that crossed his face, couldn't resist adding, 'Unless you'd prefer to keep her?'

He looked so startled that she threw back her head and laughed. And very soon Angus had joined in. His customers all paused their shopping and turned to look.

'Angus . . . ' a lady with a shopping basket declared, looking shocked. 'I don't think I've ever heard you laugh like that in all the years I've known you.'

'Blame Maxine,' he said, keeping eye contact as he smiled at her. 'She's a bad influence.'

Maxine didn't mind taking the blame. If being a bad influence made him laugh like that, then maybe she should try it more often.

★   ★   ★

Angus arrived on her doorstep again that evening, just as soon as he had closed his shop. Maxine was busy trying to update the blog on her website with information about her foster kitten.

'Any news?' he asked.

'Afraid not. Sabrina's going to spread the word around town, and my web posting's had a few views and comments, so hopefully we'll find something out soon.'

Despite Maxine having told him all she knew, he seemed in no hurry to leave.

'You could always go upstairs and check on Lucky,' she suggested when his hovering started to get in the way of her concentration.

'Lucky?'

'The kitten you found. I decided to name her Lucky — because she was lucky you found her.'

He shook his head. 'Doesn't naming her mean that you're taking ownership?'

That was very perceptive of him. The small bundle of fur had worked her way into Maxine's heart already.

'I can't have thirteen cats,' she said looking around and thinking she might be able to squeeze Lucky in somehow — she was such a tiny wee thing. 'I have no idea how she would react to this lot — or they to her. The dynamics in the place could change completely. Besides, thirteen is an unlucky number — and we've already established that she's a fortunate feline.'

He smiled and turned and headed for the stairs to check on the kitten.

'I wouldn't say no to a cup of your hot chocolate when I get back down,' he called over his shoulder.

'Cheek,' she shouted back. But she didn't mind, not really — Angus was becoming a good friend as well as a good neighbour.

As she watched him go, she wondered what was going on in that handsome head of his. Did he see her as a friend and neighbour? Or was there maybe something more behind his wanting to hang around with her, drinking hot chocolate, despite having established Lucky was fine?

⋆   ⋆   ⋆

Lucky slept on Maxine's bed that night. And, when it was time to go down to the café to take care of her cats the next morning, she decided to take the kitten with her. Just to see how her lot would

94

react to a possible new addition.

Not that she would leave the little kitten alone with her older cats. Not until Lucky had grown a little, in any case. But it wouldn't do any harm to see how they might get on.

'Now you must be a good girl,' she told Lucky as she put her down on the floor — even while knowing the little cat's sweet nature wouldn't allow anything else to happen.

Gladys was the first to approach her. 'I have my eye on you, my girl. You must be gentle,' Maxine told the older kitten. 'Lucky is very small.'

Within minutes, Lucky was following Gladys around the place as though they had been lifelong friends. And when Gladys curled up in the warmest corner for a morning snooze, Lucky curled up right beside her.

Maxine smiled. This might just work out, after all.

★　★　★

Another night on Maxine's bed, and Lucky has established herself as a part of the café family.

It had been a big mistake to allow that to happen, Maxine realised when a woman brought her two young daughters to the door before the café opened that morning.

'We saw your blog post,' the mother said. 'We only collected her from the farm up the road a couple of days ago. I went to take in a parcel from the postman and she ran out. We didn't think we'd ever see her again. The girls have been distraught.'

'How do I know she's yours?' It wasn't in Maxine's nature to be suspicious, but in her heart she knew she had to ask the question for Lucky's sake. She had been landed with the responsibility of taking care of her and couldn't possibly allow the tiny kitten to go home with a strange family without checking them out first.

'Her name's Ayesha,' one of the little girls offered. 'After the kitten in *Everyday Kittens*.'

'That's our favourite TV show,' the other little girl added helpfully.

Maxine wasn't convinced. Ayesha in *Everyday Kittens* was black, while this kitten was a grey tabby.

'I know, look at these,' the mother said, seeming to sense Maxine's doubt as she rummaged in her bag and emerged with her phone. 'We have photos.' She scrolled through and showed Maxine a series of photos of the kitten in question with various members of the family.

Her heart sank. There was no doubt that this was Lucky's family. She smiled bravely. 'I had to check.'

'Of course. I would have done the same.'

'She wasn't chipped, so we had no idea how to find you.'

'The vet suggested waiting a little while because she's so small,' the woman continued, 'but we'll be making sure that she gets chipped as soon as possible, so this doesn't happen again.'

Maxine nodded, satisfied that this family were the rightful and responsible owners she would want for Lucky. She gave the kitten one last cuddle.

Even though she knew it was the right thing, even though the joy on the faces of the two small children lifted her heart, she still felt a sharp pang of loss when she handed the little cat over.

Gladys gave a pitiful meow as Maxine came back into the café empty handed. 'I know, my darling. I'm going to miss her, too.'

⋆ ⋆ ⋆

Angus's shop was mercifully empty of customers when she went in to see him after Sabrina had arrived to open up the café. She was glad — she didn't think she could have faced anyone else just now.

'What's wrong?' he asked as he saw her face.

'I thought you might like an update.' She wiped her eyes with a tissue before quickly pushing it into her pocket. 'Lucky's gone.'

'Escaped?'

She shook her head and quickly told him about her visitors.

'Even though I still have my own cats — and even though she was barely there for any time at all — the place still feels empty without her.'

She felt bad as Angus stared awkwardly at her, so obviously unaccustomed to female tears.

'I just thought you should know as you were the one who found her,' she added. Then she headed for the door before she could embarrass herself any further by sobbing her heart out on his shoulder.

⋆　⋆　⋆

'You were right. It's for the best,' she told Angus, more for her benefit than for his, when he came around to see how she was doing after closing time. She needed to convince herself of the wisdom of those words. 'I don't have room for another cat.'

Though that wasn't true. Lucky had fitted in seamlessly — into the café and into the lives of those who lived there.

'It's so daft.' She pulled a tissue out of her pocket and began to sniff into it. 'How could I have fallen in love with her already? She was barely here.' She felt strong arms around her as she sobbed, and she leaned gratefully against his chest.

'She was a cute wee thing,' he agreed. 'Would you be cross if I told you I phoned the farm this morning after you came round to see me — the one where they said they got the cat from?'

'You did?' Her eyes narrowed as she wondered where this was heading. Had the farmer confirmed that the family who had collected Lucky — Ayesha, she corrected herself — were imposters? Might she be able to get her back? 'What did they say?'

He sighed and hugged her a little tighter. 'They said they have another kitten left, looking for a home,' he told her quietly. 'She's exactly the same colouring as Lucky.'

'Why are you telling me this?'

'I told the farmer about you — and about how upset you were when Lucky went away.'

'Ayesha,' she corrected. 'Her name's Ayesha.'

He smiled. 'She'll always be Lucky to us.'

That was true.

'Anyway, he says he'll reserve the kitten — Lucky's sister. She's yours if you want her. I know she won't replace Lucky — but maybe you could fall in love with this new kitten, too.'

She really didn't need another kitten — couldn't justify getting another one. And, as he'd pointed out, this new kitten wouldn't be Lucky. And yet she was suddenly overjoyed at the prospect and nothing made more sense.

Standing on tiptoe, she kissed him full on the mouth. When she pulled away, he looked surprised, but not displeased.

She was too delighted to be embarrassed

by her overt display of affection. She couldn't believe he'd been so thoughtful. For someone who had at their first meeting professed a dislike of cats, he seemed to understand exactly how she had felt at loosing Lucky.

'Why would you do that for me?'

'I brought her here. It was my fault you fell in love with her.'

She gave him a watery smile.

'We could go up there now,' he suggested. 'Just to see. You don't have to take her . . . '

Though really there was no question. She knew even before she'd met her that a lucky thirteenth would soon be joining her family. She nodded and went to get her coat.

As she made her way outside, she realised Angus had started to mean a good deal to her. He was definitely more than a neighbour — and even more than a friend, she realised. She wondered if he felt the same way about her.

Maybe it was time she found out.

6

Just Good Neighbours

Maxine couldn't believe that any driver would have left her delivery of cat foot outside on the pavement in the rain. Yet here were a pallet-worth of boxes getting seriously drenched.

'Need a hand with those?' a familiar voice sounded from behind her as she was calculating how best to move them, and her heart fluttered.

She turned and grinned at him. 'Please.' Having Angus next door was becoming just too handy.

He made quick work of scooping the boxes up and followed her into the café.

'They'll be fine right here, thank you, Angus.' Maxine pulled off her rain-splattered hood and pointed to a corner of the porch.

'I can take them inside if you want.

They're heavy.' He was as gruff as ever, but she appreciated his offer of help and really didn't want to take advantage.

Angus had saved her day, as he had a habit of doing. She would have had to make at least two tips, if not three.

'Here will be great, thanks. I don't want to keep you from your shop. Honestly, I don't know what that delivery driver was thinking, leaving all this cat food outside on the pavement in the rain. It wasn't as though there was nobody in — Sabrina and I are both here.'

She was going to have words with the company, just as soon as she'd dried herself and the boxes.

'You know . . . ' He hesitated.

'Yes?'

'Well I don't want this to sound as though I'm trying to hijack trade from another business, but I could order this brand in for you.'

She nodded slowly. 'That would be brilliant, but they do give me a discount because I buy in bulk ... ' Her background in accounts meant she knew how important it was for a small business to keep a close eye on cash flow — and how easy it was to go under when you forgot to do that.

As a new venture, her café wouldn't easily be able to absorb the loss of the discount. Though she didn't want to push it. She knew that Angus's grocer's shop was being squeezed financially by the out-of-town supermarket everyone seemed to be going to.

'No problem.' He brushed a lock of hair, still damp from the rain, back from his forehead. 'How about I let you have them at cost?'

'I couldn't possibly let you do that.'

'Of course you can. Neighbours have to help each other out.' His face broke into the briefest of smiles before he turned and left.

She gave in to her own urge to smile as she secured the door behind him, before taking the first of the boxes so she could put the order away.

She'd barely stepped into the café before she was besieged by a crowd of cats — tackled from every direction. Sadie, her newest little tabby, leapt to perch majestically atop the box in her hand. A handful of other felines became tangled in her feet as she walked. Gladys, being the cheekiest of the lot, ended up on her shoulder.

'Hey,' she told the Norwegian forest cat, 'you're getting way too big for that kind of nonsense.'

Sabrina smiled as she swept towards them, moving quickly to pick Gladys up and put her in a place of safety on her lap. 'That was nice of Angus,' she said, opening a conversation Maxine was keen to have.

'It was.' Maxine perched at one of the café's tables for a moment. 'The problem I have with Angus,' she said, even though Sabrina hadn't asked, 'is that he's always rushing around to be my knight in shining armour.'

'How is that a problem?' Sabrina finished brushing Gladys and lifted the cat onto the floor. 'I mean, surely that's the ideal scenario — a neighbour who's happy to be useful.'

Maxine sighed. She liked Angus a lot, but she couldn't see the relationship going anywhere while things were so one-sided. 'I suppose you're right.'

Sabrina's eyes narrowed. 'So what exactly is your problem here?'

'The trouble is,' Maxine continued, setting Sadie down on the floor so she could put her order away, 'that he's taken time out of his shop to help me here at the cat café and he's never lets me pay for his time.'

'I should imagine he hasn't.' Sabrina picked up Brian, the next cat on today's feline grooming list, and began to brush. 'How would you feel if you did some-one a favour and they suddenly mentioned they wanted to give you money?'

Maxine wouldn't like it at all. She had the good grace to admit that to herself, even if she wasn't about to let her employee in on the secret. She decided to treat Sabrina's question as rhetorical and continued moving boxes — conveniently forgetting that she was the one who had initially mentioned the problem.

'You know what you need to do?' Sabrina asked when everything was safely stored away, obviously not quite ready to let the subject go. 'You need to find some way to be neighbourly in return.'

That was easier said than done. It wasn't as though she hadn't already been looking for a chance to repay him for his help.

'I'll give it some thought,' she said, as she glanced towards the window. The first group of pre-booked visitors of the day were already queuing up outside. 'But for now, we'd better open the café.'

Things were going well with the café. Every session was full today, and Maxine didn't get a moment to herself. Even so, even with all those distractions, it was difficult to get thoughts of the man next door out of her head.

'What about cooking Angus a nice dinner to thank him for his help?' Sabrina suggested as she was leaving that night. It seemed she'd been mulling over Maxine's problem all day, too.

'Maybe.' In theory, it was a good idea, but . . .

Maxine frowned as she locked up behind her assistant.

What she hadn't told Sabrina was that Angus had already made her a meal — and there was no point her trying to make him something special because he was a much better cook than she was.

* * *

Over the next few weeks, Maxine kept a close eye out for some way she could redress the balance. Nevertheless, she seemed to always be the one who needed a helping hand. She wasn't used to playing the helpless female, but sometimes even the most independent of women needed a man's brute strength. As with the delivery the other day, for example. And, every single time he helped her, it meant he was neglecting his own shop — even if he refused to acknowledge it.

She couldn't keep away from him, though, and usually found some excuse to pop into his shop during the day.

Then one day, a few weeks after the cat-food-in-the-rain near catastrophe, she went to buy a pint of milk and she knew at one there was something wrong. Angus barely smiled when she walked in; instead, he seemed to be frowning at a mountain of paperwork as he stood behind the till. She hadn't seen him this grumpy since the day she'd told him she was opening a cat café next door to his shop.

Trying not to take his lack of greeting personally, she picked up the milk, and on impulse a packet of biscuits, and took them to the till.

With a sigh, he tidied the paperwork away into a carrier bag before ringing through her shopping. 'Accounts,' he said with a grimace. 'I hate doing them.'

Maxine smiled. 'Most people do. And thank goodness for that, because that's what kept me in a work before I opened up next door.'

For some of her colleagues, accountancy had been their life's calling — a career they had wholeheartedly embraced. For Maxine, though, it had never been more than just a job. Despite qualifying and doing her very best, her heart hadn't been in it. Not the way her heart was in her cat café.

Though, as she glanced at Angus, she realised that maybe she now wanted more than just the cats and her café.

Maybe she should just ask him out. Even if her career-woman brain required her to be on an equal footing, her romantic heart just longed for him to take her in his arms.

'Are you busy this evening?' he asked before she could say anything.

'I've no plans,' she said, trying to breathe normally as their eyes met and his hand brushed against hers as he dropped her change into her palm. 'Why?'

'As you just pointed out, you're an accountant.'

'I *was* an accountant.'

'Well, if you're free, I could do with some help.' He nodded towards the bag of receipts and invoices.

She smiled. It might not be the romantic date she'd hoped she might one day share with Angus, but she couldn't have been more delighted that the tables were turning. At last he needed her help.

'Get everything together and bring it through to the café after closing time. I'll have a look and see what I can do.' She smiled.

OK, so she'd been mistaken that he was going to ask her out, but there would be time to explore the possibility of a romance after his books had been balanced.

★　★　★

'It's not a date,' Maxine insisted after making the mistake of telling Sabrina what had happened.

112

Sabrina didn't look convinced. 'Well if it isn't, it should be. You two are made for each other. Are you sure Angus isn't using his accounts as an excuse? Maybe he's trying any means to get closer.'

She thought about it for a minute, then quickly dismissed the notion. Angus was the plainest-speaking man she'd ever met. She was sure he wouldn't have an ulterior motive.

'It's difficult to get romantic over a profit and loss account. If that's his plan, he's seriously misguided.'

Besides, Maxine had seen the state of his paperwork — all scrunched up into a carrier bag, for heaven's sake. No, Angus was a man in genuine need, and even though she quite fancied the idea that he might make an excuse to spend time with her, she was sure that wasn't the case.

*   *   *

If Maxine had doubted his motives for a moment, Angus's business-like air when he turned up at her place that evening confirmed her hypothesis; this was nothing remotely like a date.

'Do you always leave your paperwork in this state?' she asked as she got stuck in. 'It would be easier if you just did it as you went along instead of letting it build up.'

He shrugged a broad shoulder and sat down. Without missing a beat, he immediately became a person of interest to the feline population of the café. Maxine bit back a smile. He seemed resigned, though, and didn't even try to move Alfie from his lap, or Gladys from his shoulder.

'What will I do?' he asked. 'To help.'

'Put those cats down, then you can go and make me a cup of tea,' she said. 'Then you can go back to your plac,e and I should have the numbers for you by tomorrow morning.'

He brought her tea through to the café and set it down at the table she'd set up as a work desk. He seemed reluctant to leave.

114

She looked up and saw that he'd brought a cup through for himself, too. She was inexplicably pleased by that. It wasn't that she didn't like being on her own with her cats, but it was nice to have some human company in the evening for a change.

Even if all that human company did was sit in brooding silence as she sifted through receipts and reconciled bank accounts.

★ ★ ★

It was getting late by the time Maxine finalised the numbers. 'It's not looking good,' she told him frankly. She'd seen it before, small business run into the ground by large local competition. She was sure the fault could be laid firmly at the door of the large out-of-town shopping centre.

'I had gathered,' he said dryly. 'Customers can be thin on the ground these days.'

'You need to budget,' she told him.

115

'You're holding too much stock for the level of sales.'

He nodded.

'And you could diversify. Can you specialise in something? Become a delicatessen? Or import chocolates? You need to provide something unique — give people a reason to visit you.' Maybe she was overstepping the mark, but as a qualified accountant, she was accustomed to giving business advice.

Luckily, Angus didn't seem in the least offended. 'Like you've done here with the cat café?'

She looked around at her sleepy felines. 'Well, yes. I suppose I have done that. Though really, my business plan was driven more by my heart than my head. You couldn't do something like this unless you were passionate about cats. It's just my good luck that lots of other people love them, too.'

He nodded. 'You've got a good business going here.'

'And you could have a good business, too.'

'I had been thinking I might go back to being an electrician.'

She gave a mental shudder, imagining how she would be feeling if it was suggested she should give up the cat café and go back to accountancy.

'Is that what you want to do?'

He shrugged. A sleepy Gladys who had settled there gave a lazy meow, and he reached and scratched behind her ear.

'In an ideal world, no. Doesn't seem I have much choice, though.'

'There's always a choice.'

'When my wife Jessie left, I felt I needed a complete change. That was why I gave up what was considered to be a good job and took over the shop.'

She nodded sympathetically. She could understand the urge to leave an unhappy past behind and start anew.

'What happened?' she asked, and was immediately appalled that she'd been so inquisitive. It was none of her business — and she waited Angus to tell her so. But he didn't.

'She met someone else.' He was quiet for a moment. 'Can't say I blame her. I can be a bit of a misery at times.'

'No you're not.' Maxine shook her head. 'In fact, I think you're wonderful.' She immediately felt her face warm — why had she said that?

Their eyes met, and for just a moment, she suspected he was going to lean across and kiss her. She held her breath. But then the moment passed.

'I'll look out for your bill,' he said with a smile that made her heart lurch.

There wouldn't be a bill, of course. But now didn't seem the time to tell him that.

★　★　★

'Well?' Sabrina demanded when she arrived the next day. 'How was your non-date with Angus?'

'Exactly as you'd expect a non-date to be.' Maxine smiled, hugging the details of the shared confidences and the almost-kisses to herself. The first was none of Sabrina's business — and neither was the second.

'You two are as useless as each other.' Sabrina shook her head as she went off to get the cleaning materials to prepare the café for opening.

'Quite possibly we are,' Maxine admitted.

★ ★ ★

'I've been waiting for your bill,' Angus called across the shop without pre-amble the next time Maxine went in. 'My accountant tells me I need to budget, so I need to know how much I'm going to have to pay her.'

She shook her head. 'There's no bill. You've done so much to help me since I moved in,' she said. 'In fact, I don't know how I'd have managed without you, so this is the very least I can do.'

His smile faded and he sighed. 'I didn't ask you to help because I wanted my books done free of charge.'

'I know that.' She ignored the lure of

her shopping list and approached the counter where he stood.

'It's not a competition, you know.' His voice was softer now, his eyes fixed on her face as he spoke.

'What isn't?'

'Being a good neighbour.'

She sighed. 'If it was a competition, you'd be winning by a mile.'

'We all do what we can.'

She nodded, seizing on his words. 'And I can do the books for your shop.' He didn't like it; she could see it in his frown. 'That's what good neighbours do, they help each other out,' she told him softly. 'And that's what friends do, too.'

Suddenly she felt so much better. Accepting help wasn't a sign of weakness — it was a mark of friendship every bit as much as offering help was.

He smiled awkwardly. 'Would it interest you to know that finding ways to help you out has actually become the highlight of my day?'

Her heart leapt. 'Yes — that would

interest me a lot.'

He took her hand. She gave his fingers an encouraging squeeze.

'How about, if you don't want to bill me, you let me take you out to dinner? Somewhere nice, where we can get dressed up in smart clothes and make an evening of it? Maybe go dancing afterwards?'

'Angus, just so we're clear, will this dancing be just a way to say thank you for me doing your books? Because it sounds like you might be asking me out on a date.'

She might seem pretty clueless that she needed to ask — but she preferred that to misconstruing the situation and embarrassing herself. Besides, he'd invited her for a meal before. He'd cooked Christmas lunch for her when they had both planned to spend the day alone. Though it had been very enjoyable, there had been nothing romantic about it.

The way he looked into her eyes now, though, was *very* romantic. All at once, she didn't care if she made a fool of herself. She wanted to tell him that yes, she would have dinner with him. She just wanted to spend more time with him. She wanted to go with him onto the dance floor and dance in his arms until dawn.

She could feel her heart racing as she waited for his reply.

'If I was suggesting a date, would you say yes, Maxine?'

And she dared to breathe. 'Yes.' She couldn't seem to stop smiling as she nodded her agreement. 'I'd like that.'

'Good.' His grin made her breath catch. 'Because I'd like it, too.'

7

First Date

'I'm sorry, my darling, but you're going to have to move.' Maxine carefully lifted Gladys from her perch on the computer keyboard and placed her on the floor.

'Mew,' Gladys objected.

'Yes, I know it's inconvenient,' Maxine said, 'but I have to check the bookings to see who we're expecting.'

Another twelve pairs of feline eyes stared accusingly at Maxine, annoyed their sister had been disturbed. Meanwhile, Sabrina smiled at the scene before turning her attention to shaking cushions and straightening chairs, ready for their first group of guests.

It was going to be a busy session — they were fully booked, which was exactly how Maxine liked it. She smiled. Her life was going from good to even better. Her cat café was thriving — and her relationship with Angus from next door was teetering on the brink of romance, with a proper date planned at last.

The first group of excited visitors trooped in — some regular, some new — and Maxine quickly went through the house rules that were designed to protect the welfare of the cats.

'Please don't pick them up,' she reeled off her list. 'And please keep your cakes and snacks away from them.' Given half a chance, they would make off with any tasty crumb — and that would make a mockery of the balanced feline diet she'd carefully devised.

'Atishoo.'

The sudden sound reverberated around the café, silencing Maxine as staff, customers, and cats looked around in surprise.

Maxine was the first to recover her wits. 'Bless you, Hester,' she called, hoping her breezy manner would lessen the guest's obvious embarrassment.

Really, they should all be used to Hester Carmichael's sneezing by now.

The woman had quickly become one of the cat café's regular customers and generally popped by at least once a week, bringing with her a raging allergy to cat hair.

'It's worth the risk,' she'd said with a laugh when Maxine had expressed concern. 'It would be too much to live with cat hair on a permanent basis, but a quick visit now and then won't do me any harm.'

'But . . . ' Maxine had started to object, not wanting her café to be the source of discomfort to anyone.

Hester had held up her hand to stop the conversation stone dead in its tracks. 'Could you live in a world without cat cuddles?' she'd asked, holding Maxine's worried gaze.

Maxine knew when she was defeated. She had no choice but to leave the decision to Hester, trusting the customer knew best about matters involving her own health.

The answer to Hester's question was simple. No, Maxine could not imagine a life without cats. Not now, at least. Though circumstances — in the form of a busy job and a cat resistant fiancé — had once made owning a cat impossible, so she had instant sympathy for Hester's plight.

If she could make things easier for Hester and brighten her life, then she was happy to help. After all, that was the main reason she had started her business — to spread the joy of cats far and wide. Particularly to those who might not be able to keep a pet of their own for whatever reason.

'Sorry about that,' Hester said now, fishing in her pocket for a tissue before blowing her nose. 'I can't imagine why I'm reacting so badly today.' She sniffed loudly, her eyes very obviously beginning to water.

Maxine frowned. This wasn't looking good.

'I hope your allergy's not getting worse,' Sabrina finally dared to voice the concern.

'Don't say that,' Hester pleaded

before sneezing again.

A dozen feline faces watched warily from a safe distance. But the thirteenth cat spotted her chance — Gladys, not in the least deterred, immediately leapt onto the guest's lap. Judging by the smiles that ensued, Maxine guessed Hester considered this a minor inconvenience. Which was just as well, as she was immediately forced to find another tissue to dab at her watery eyes.

'Maybe you'll feel better if you nip outside for a minute or two?' Maxine suggested, sure all that was needed was a blast of fresh air to make the guest more comfortable.

Hester nodded, gently lifting Gladys to the floor before making her way to the door, sneezing as she went.

She was still in a sorry state when Maxine went out to check on her a few minutes later. 'How about you go home for today,' she suggested gently. 'And I'll rebook your session for later in the week. What about Friday? I'll make it first thing. We always give the place a good clean before we open, so there will be fewer cat hairs around.' Though that hadn't helped today, sadly.

'Thanks, Maxine.'

'Poor Hester,' Sabrina said later, after all the customers had left and they were cleaning and tidying ready for closing. 'I can't imagine how it must be to love cats so much, but to be so allergic to them.'

'Nature can be cruel,' Maxine agreed.

They worked quietly for a few minutes, both subdued as they each considered Hester's plight.

'Let's talk about something a bit more cheerful,' Sabrina suggested, and Maxine's heart sank a little further. She didn't need to ask what subject her assistant had in mind. 'At least you have your date with Angus to look forward to on Friday.'

Sabrina grinned and Maxine had to forcibly stop herself from sighing. Ever since she had confessed that she and Angus — after much flirting and dancing around the issue — had formally arranged to go an actual date, Sabrina had turned the conversation around to the subject at almost every opportunity. Not that she minded talking about Angus as such, but she didn't want her assistant reading too much into a simple night out.

'Yes,' she said calmly, determined not to be drawn into the conversation any further than she had to be. 'At least I have that to look forward to.'

Her previous failed engagement had made her cautious. But her friendship with Angus had crept up on her — and, before she'd even been aware, there was the possibility of a whole lot more.

'What are you going to wear?' Sabrina asked, determined not to let the subject go and straightening up the chairs and cushions as she spoke.

'I think I might run out after we've finished up here, and buy something.' Instantly she realised she should have kept quiet. She had revealed too much without thinking.

Sabrina's eyebrows ended up in her

hairline. 'You're going to buy a new outfit? For your date with Angus? That makes me think you're maybe a bit more serious about this than you're letting on?'

Maxine realised that maybe it was too late now to try playing it cool.

'Apart from at my wedding,' Sabrina continued, 'I've never seen you wear anything other than your uniform.'

Maxine looked down at the jeans and cat motif T-shirt she wore to work these days. It was going to be nice to get dressed up. She smiled, deciding to embrace her friend's excitement for this night out.

After all, half the fun of a first date was the anticipation.

'He's gone to a lot of trouble to make arrangements,' Maxine said, struggling not to sound defensive.

Angus had booked a table for two in the most exclusive restaurant in town. And the possibility of dancing had been mentioned. She guessed that for a man like Angus, that had taken a lot of effort.

The least she could do was to dress up nicely.

* * *

The next morning, a sliver of early morning light broke through a crack in the curtain and gently persuaded Maxine to open her eyes.

Her gaze immediately fell on the new dress hanging on the wardrobe door, ready for her date with Angus. Red and frivolous, it was a complete departure for Maxine in the fashion department. But surely a date with a man she liked very much warranted such a fuss.

It seemed she wasn't the only one awake at this early hour, she realised as she became aware that the weight that had been asleep on her feet had stirred and was moving on the duvet. She wasn't surprised when she found herself nose to nose with a feline face.

Ever since Angus had taken Maxine to pick the little cat up from the farm, this had been Sadie's normal way of announcing she was ready for breakfast.

'Meow,' she added, in case Maxine hadn't taken the hint.

'Good morning, my darling,' Maxine croaked in reply, aware that her throat was decidedly scratchy. She sat up, pulling the little tabby up with her, and ruffling behind the cat's ears. She was rewarded with a contented purr. 'I think I could do with a cup of tea while I'm preparing your food.'

She sounded nothing like herself, and a nice hot drink was bound to help.

The phone was ringing in the café by the time she'd carried Sadie downstairs and filled the kettle. No doubt it would be a customer. Maxine was tempted to let it go to the answering machine so she could deal with it later, but some impulse made her pick the call up.

'Maxine, it's Hester. I hope I didn't wake you.'

Maxine was glad the other woman had announced herself, because she would have been hard pushed to have made out who it was. Hester's voice was practically unrecognisable.

'You don't sound at all well, Hester.'

'I'm not. The sneezing the other day — it wasn't my allergy after all. I have a cold.' She sneezed loudly for good measure. 'Actually, it's more than a cold — though maybe not quite flu. I'm afraid I'll need to cancel that rescheduled visit. I don't want to spread my germs.'

Too late to worry about that, Maxine thought ruefully. It was blatantly obvious now why her own throat was sore.

'I'm sorry to hear that,' she said with genuine sympathy. 'Let me know when you're feeling better and we can rebook that visit.'

'Thank you so much, Maxine. I really appreciate that.'

The kettle had boiled by the time she'd finished the call, but Maxine decided to forgo the tea and she poured herself a large glass of orange juice instead. She needed vitamin C to ward off this cold. She wasn't going to succumb — she refused to be ill. She was looking forward to this date tomorrow night way too much to let anything ruin it.

★ ★ ★

'Sabrina, can you cope on your own down here if I work on the accounts upstairs?' Even though she was adamant her symptoms would come to nothing, Maxine didn't want to mingle with her visitors until she'd seen off her sore throat.

'Of course.' Sabrina was happy to help, but Maxine could see her concerned frown. 'Will you be OK for tomorrow?' she asked. 'For your date with Angus.'

'I'll be fine.' Maxine was determined. Nothing was going to ruin the evening.

Sabrina supplied Maxine with orange juice as she kept herself hidden upstairs in the flat, with Gladys and Sadie keeping her company.

'That's the last of the orange,' she reported as she brought up a snack at lunchtime. 'I'll just pop next door and get some more.'

'No, I'll go.' Maxine smiled, I'm feeling better 'And I could do with the change of scenery.'

Though she wished she hadn't caught a glimpse of herself in the mirror in the hallway on the way out. She looked a wreck.

'All set for tomorrow night?' Angus asked when he saw her.

'Dancing shoes dusted and raring to go,' she replied, hoping her nose wasn't letting her down with its cold induced redness. If it was, Angus wasn't letting on.

'I'm glad to hear it. My dancing shoes are ready, too.' As he held her gaze, his frown melted away into a heart-stopping smile.

His attention turned to her wire basket of shopping. 'Have the café customers suddenly acquired a taste for orange juice?' he asked as he rang her many cartons through the till.

'No, it's for me. I'm feeling OK,' which was true even if she didn't look

135

it, 'but as a precaution I thought it wise to top up my vitamin C levels to fight off the cold germs that are doing the rounds.'

Quickly she told him the story of Hester and the cold that had masqueraded as an allergy.

'Why would someone visit a cat café if they're allergic to cats?' He seemed genuinely perplexed, and Maxine bit back a smile. There was still a way to go before Angus's conversion to crazy cat neighbour would be complete. His reaction now proved that.

'Because she really loves cats.'

Angus shook his head as he put Maxine's shopping into her bag. 'How can someone love something that causes them harm?'

Maxine smiled. 'How can she not when it's cats?'

He laughed. 'You'd have thought they might have invented a hypoallergenic cat by now, the things they can do with science.'

Angus had only meant it as a jokey

comment, but his words set something ticking in Maxine's brain. Slowly she smiled as she realised she'd had the answer to Hester's problem all along.

'Angus,' she told him, 'you're a genius.'

His frown was back in place. 'I am?'

'Yes, you are.'

When she'd been researching cat cafés, when she'd still only been hoping to open her own, she'd travelled the country, visiting everyone one she could find. There hadn't been many. But one in particular was called to mind now. They'd had a pair of gorgeous Sphynx cats. If Hester was allergic to cat hair, then she would be fine with that breed — because those two cats hadn't had a single hair between them.

She would ring Hester and make the suggestion as soon as she got back to her flat. And she'd give Angus full credit. It was only fair.

★ ★ ★

'You look dreadful,' Sabrina said when Maxine let her into the café the next morning.

'Thanks.'

'Go for a nap,' she ordered. 'And don't even think of doing any more paperwork today.'

'I'm fine.' She wasn't really, though. Hester had been right — this was definitely more than a cold. 'Well, I'll maybe have a quick disco nap so I'm refreshed for my night out,' she finally conceded.

That would do the trick nicely. It would have to, because she would have to be OK for her date tonight. It had taken so long for her and Angus to arrange to go on this date, she was worried that this might be their only chance.

If proof were needed that she wasn't herself, Sadie — who would normally take every opportunity to race up to the flat whenever Maxine went there — seemed reluctant to join her.

'Do I look that bad?' she asked the little tabby.

138

'You look fine.' Sabrina ushered her towards the hall so she could go up to the flat. 'Sadie just wants to stay and play with her friends. Now do you want me to pop next door and tell Angus you're not well enough to go out tonight?'

'No.' She shocked herself by just about shouting. 'I'm sorry, Sabrina, I didn't mean to snap — but I'm sure I'll be fine by this evening. I'm sure your suggestion of a nap will do the trick.'

★   ★   ★

She awoke to the sound of a man's voice in her living room. Glancing at the bedside clock, she saw it was late.

'Angus,' she muttered as she got out of bed and pulled on her dressing gown.

It was past their meeting time; she couldn't believe she'd slept all afternoon and into the evening.

'I'm so sorry,' she said as she burst from the bedroom, tying the belt of her

dressing gown as she went, to find
Sabrina and Angus. He was so handsome in his suit; she couldn't believe
she'd ruined their date.

'What are you sorry for?' he asked.

'For standing you up.' She turned to
Sabrina. 'For leaving you alone in the
café all day.'

'It was all fine,' Sabrina assured her.
'You couldn't help being ill. Angus just
wanted to pop up to see how you were
— I explained to him that I didn't think
you'd make it to dinner.'

'No,' she agreed, realising with a
sinking heart the truth of that statement.

'Now you're up, I'd best be going.'
Sabrina slipped the strap of her bag
over her shoulder. 'Chloe will be
needing a lift to her swimming class.'

'Thanks, Sabrina, for everything. I'll
see you tomorrow.'

The cat minder gave a little wave of
acknowledgment as she went.

'How *are* you feeling?' Angus asked
once they were alone. '*Really?*'

140

'Better.' She was surprised to find she meant it. Sleep had done its job. 'Though maybe not dinner-and-dancing better. And I must look a mess.'

He took a step closer. 'You look beautiful.' He looked a bit embarrassed by the admission, but her heart leapt because she knew he never said anything he didn't mean.

'I'm sorry,' she told him again. 'Our dinner . . . '

'There will be other dinners.'

'Are you sure?'

'Positive.' He took another step closer.

'But it was our first date and I've ruined it.'

'We can still have our first date. We can watch a film and order a pizza — that's if you feel up to it.'

'But the dancing . . . ' She'd been so looking forward to it. And she hoped he had been, too.

Hesitantly, he reached out and took her hand. 'We can dance right here.'

She was practically breathless with

anticipation as he drew her even closer, his eyes fixed on hers. She was sure he was going to kiss her.

At the last moment, she turned her head so his lips landed on her ear. 'Germs,' she whispered. 'I don't want you to be ill, too.'

He laughed softly. 'I'm willing to take my chances,' he said. 'If that's OK with you.'

He was grinning when she turned back to face him.

'If it's OK with you, it's fine by me.' And she leaned closer, closed her eyes, and she and her germs kissed him before he could change his mind.

8

Birthday Wishes

Things were going well, Maxine reflected as she picked up her purse and her shopping bag. Her café was becoming established, and she was forging new friendships. But none meant more to her than the relationship she was teetering on the brink of with the man next door.

Angus smiled full beam as Maxine walked into his shop. Her step faltered as her gaze met his. 'Hi,' she said, her heart fluttering madly. She told it to stop. It seemed to be fluttering with unnecessary regularity these days — particularly whenever Angus was around.

They might be spending a lot of time in each other's company, they might have even been out on a date or two, but they'd both agreed to keep things casual.

It was safer that way. And fluttering heartbeats were definitely venturing into dangerous territory. She didn't want to risk a broken heart and another failed engagement, however much she might like him.

'Happy birthday, Maxine,' he said softly as she approached the counter and paused at the point where the wire baskets were stacked.

'Thank you.' She'd only mentioned her birthday to him once in passing, and that had been weeks ago. She was touched he'd remembered. Her ex-fiancé hadn't — not once in the five years they'd dated. And she hadn't been inclined to remind him.

'Doing anything special today?'

She shook her head. 'Normal working day for me.' But as her working day was filled with cats and chatting to lovely customers at her café, that was no hardship. Then she added, almost as an afterthought: 'Though I am going to be making a birthday cake this morning before the café opens for business. I looked up the recipe online.'

He nodded thoughtfully, before his expression sobered. 'Should you be making your own cake? That doesn't seem right.'

She knew she should tell him the truth about this particular cake, but she could only guess at the reaction. He was bound to think she was daft.

So she smiled in what she hoped was a mysterious manner, picked up a basket, and made her way to the shelves. She really was very happy with her life — though she'd worked hard to make it into everything it was now.

And it didn't really matter that she wasn't going to make a birthday cake for herself. At her age, birthdays meant very little now. And ever since her father had died, there had been nobody left to make a fuss of her special day — her friends had all been serious people, concentrating on work rather than frivolities.

With a sigh, she turned her thoughts to her shopping list.

145

Flour, she read the first item. Of course, a cake recipe, however unusual, called for flour.

She lifted a bag of self-raising from the shelf and put it into her basket. And she needed eggs. And cheese. And not forgetting the most important ingredient of all for this extra-special birthday cake — a tin of tuna.

'Making sandwiches for your visitors now?' Angus asked as he rang her purchases through the till. 'Is it wise to offer tuna as a filling with that lot you have next door? They're bad enough going after the cupcakes and gateaux. I can see them knocking tuna sandwiches straight from your customers' hands.'

She shook her head. 'Not sandwiches. And the tuna's not for the customers.'

'Oh?' He popped the tin of tuna into her shopping bag.

She knew she couldn't hold onto her secret for much longer — not now he'd noticed and commented on that crucial ingredient. 'It's for the birthday cake.'

Silence greeted her revelation. He stared at her, his expression inscrutable. Slowly, he arched an eyebrow. 'You're putting tuna into your birthday cake? That will be tasty with a cup of tea.' His dark eyes were filled with amusement as he quickly caught up with her train of thought. 'It's not for you, is it, this cake.' It wasn't a question.

'It's for the cats,' she confirmed, and she waited for the usual reaction that would normally accompany such a statement. She was mildly disappointed when it failed to materialise. She liked it when he laughed, even if it was generally at something she'd said.

This time Angus simply nodded. 'I suppose your cats are family, so it makes sense you'd want them to join in with your birthday celebrations.'

'It's not my special day we'll be celebrating. It's Teddy's birthday today, too.' Teddy was a particularly handsome Selkirk Rex who lived at Maxine's cat café along with his twelve adopted feline siblings.

'The cake's for Teddy's birthday?' There was hardly an inflection to his tone, but Maxine sensed his surprised nonetheless.

'It's for the party later today. We'll all sing to him, then the cats will all get a tasty bite of the cake.'

'You're having a birthday party for him?'

Maxine nodded. 'I am.'

'Even though he's a cat?' The expression was deadpan, but she could feel there was a hearty burst of amusement waiting to bubble forth. She couldn't bring herself to be indignant, though. His friendship was important. Actually, she would go so far as to say the *he* was important.

'My café regulars are looking forward to it,' she said in her own defence. 'All the spaces for the party were booked within minutes of me putting them on the website.'

'Because there's nothing at all unusual in a cat having a birthday party.' Again, the same deadpan expression, but with a twinkle in his eyes — and Maxine felt the corners of her mouth twitch in response.

'Nothing at all.' Delivered in a tone that equalled his for seriousness.

'Thought not.' He packed the remainder of her shopping into her bag and finally, unable to hold his amusement in check any longer, he grinned.

'It's this evening,' she told him. 'After your shop's closing time.' Not that she'd consciously planned it that way — it was just an accident. A happy accident. 'Would you like to come?'

She wasn't sure about asking him. It wasn't as though he was as cat-mad as she was — or as the customers who had rushed to buy tickets for the party must be. But it would be nice to have him there. The cats liked him very much. And, if she was honest, so did she.

'I thought you'd sold all the slots.'

'I'm sure we can find room for you.'

'Would I have to eat the tuna cake?'

She picked up her bag. 'You would not. That's strictly for the cats. Humans will have the usual selection of cupcakes, traybakes, or gateaux to choose from.'

'In that case, I'll be there.'

'But you will have to sing happy birthday to Teddy,' she let slip — and hurried from the shop before he could recover from the shock of her parting statement.

She was still grinning as she popped back next door.

Really, if she didn't know any better, she'd swear that Angus had been actually very pleased with his invitation to Teddy's party, despite his obvious amusement at the prospect.

★ ★ ★

When he'd arrived at the café, Teddy had made short work of fitting in with the other cats, and was soon respected by the other residents — as befitted his status as both the oldest and the most assertive of the café cats. A handsome oatmeal-coloured Selkirk Rex, he needed a lot of grooming to keep his curly fur looking smart. And it was exactly that

150

curly fur that gave him both the appearance of a teddy bear and therefore his name. And, even though he would likely be oblivious to the reason for the fuss, Maxine thought it only right that he have a celebration held in his honour today.

As she let herself into the café with her purchases, she was greeted at the door by a loud meow. 'Hello to you, too, Gladys,' she told the young Norwegian Forest cat. 'I suppose you can smell the tuna even though the can hasn't even been opened yet.'

'So you got the ingredients for the cake?' Sabrina asked as Maxine made her way through the café towards the kitchen.

'I did. I think that recipe I found on the internet looks quite easy, so fingers crossed I'll manage it.'

Sabrina grinned. 'I do love working for you,' she said. 'And I completely love the cats. But making a cake for Teddy to eat on his birthday?' She shook her head. 'Is that maybe a step too far? You do know Teddy has no idea it's his birthday?'

'He'll know something's up, especially when he's offered tuna,' Maxine assured her. 'Besides, you know this is as much for us as it is for him.'

'You're daft.' Sabrina laughed.

'And, more importantly, it's for the customers.' Maxine smiled as she spoke, not in the least offended by her assistant's words, because she happened to know Sabrina was exactly as cat-mad as she was herself.

'It *is* a good way to bring customers in,' Sabrina admitted. 'Even if you hardly need to do that with the café being fully booked for most sessions.'

'A good businesswoman is always looking for new angles.' Which was all very well, but she'd never made any of her decisions in cold-hearted attempt to bring in custom. Each and every development of her café had the welfare and well-being of her cats at the centre — and her own interests some way after. That customers were attracted by those decisions was a bonus. For an ex-accountant, it was no way to run a business — but for a self-confessed crazy cat lady, she was living the dream.

'Teddy will enjoy the cake. At least I hope he will.' She frowned. 'And it's not like you haven't been encouraging me,' she reminded her assistant. 'This party was your idea.'

'That's true,' Sabrina admitted her part in this. 'Did you tell Angus about it?'

Maxine nodded.

'I'm sure he found it highly amusing.'

'Actually, he was very supportive.'

Sabrina's eyes widened.

'I know,' Maxine said, reacting to her assistant's visible shock. 'I don't know what happened, either.'

'You're not sure what happened?' Sabrina was incredulous. 'He's in love, is what's happened. In his eyes, you can do no wrong.'

'In love? Oh, no, I don't think so.' Despite her denial, her heart gave another alarming flutter.

'Don't you?' Sabrina looked amused.

Maxine sighed. She liked Angus very much. And she knew he liked her. But love was something else completely. Something that might have had the possibility of happening, given how her pulse always quickened around him, but neither of them were prepared to allow it.

'We like spending time together,' she insisted, refusing to meet Sabrina's eyes. 'And a couple of dates aren't a solid foundation for falling in love.'

It was much too soon for talk of love. And it probably always would be for the two of them. They were both set in their ways, happy with their own businesses and their own lives.

But still, he was the guest Maxine was most looking forward to seeing at the party this evening.

*   *   *

All day there was a sense of expectation in the air as guests arrived for their pre-booked slots. Word had gotten out about Teddy's birthday — probably in no small part down to Maxine's blog post — and, even though the official celebration wasn't planned until tonight, everyone who called by was pleased to see the birthday boy. Some even sang to him.

'Poor Teddy looks very unimpressed,' Sabrina said with a laugh as yet another group began a burst of 'Happy Birthday'.

It was as the café was about to re-open after their quick lunch break that Maxine noticed something amiss. 'Where's Gladys?' she asked, looking around. 'And Sadie? I haven't seen either of them for a while.'

They each began to look, and checked the cupboards and all the hidey places Maxine had installed to make sure her cats could have quiet time if needed.

'In here . . . ' Sabrina eventually called from the kitchen, the tone of her voice making Maxine dread what she might find.

'How on earth did they get in here?'

she asked as she stopped at the door and surveyed the devastation.

Despite the kitchen door being firmly closed to enforce the no-cats rule, the two of them had managed to make their way in — and they'd helped themselves to Teddy's cake.

'I should have put it in the fridge.' Maxine had left it out to cool on a wire rack and completely forgotten it.

'They've eaten it all,' Sabrina said in horror, picking up the plate and studying it as though hoping to find the missing cake magically reappearing. 'There are only a few crumbs left.'

Meanwhile, the culprits sat on the counter — a counter that would need to be disinfected pronto — and stared up at them, both the very picture of innocence.

'Oh, no.' Maxine took on a stern tone as she approached the cats. 'How could you eat your brother's cake?' There was no doubting who the ring leader was — Gladys was always at the centre of any mischief.

'What are we doing to do?' Sabrina asked. 'There's no time to make another — we're booked solid for the rest of the day.'

Maxine shuddered. She could imagine how the café guests would react if she made another cake while they were here — with the accompanying cacophony of caterwauling felines stationed at the kitchen door.

'I'll ring Angus,' she decided. 'We'll forget the cake and I'll ask him to bring a couple of tins of tuna. 'We can give them that as we sing to Teddy at the party. Though I think someone deserves no more treats today.' She glanced sternly at the furry menaces.

'Mew,' Gladys commented as she and Sadie both stared up at her. And Maxine's heart melted. How could she stay cross with those were faces?

*　*　*

Angus didn't bring the tins of tuna. He brought a perfectly made cat cake

157

instead. It was definitely more impressive than Maxine's version — he'd even decorated it with a few prawns on the top and two birthday candles. Though, of course, Teddy was only interested in the parts of the cake he could eat, and Maxine ended up blowing out the candles and making a wish for the biggest piece of cake on his behalf.

'How on earth did you manage it?' she asked once everyone had left and they were alone with the cats in the café.

'You're not the only one who can use the internet to download recipes, you know,' he told her gruffly. Though she could see he was trying not to smile.

'But how did you find the time?'

'I shut the shop early.'

'Angus — you really shouldn't have done that.'

He shrugged a broad shoulder. 'I had to shut up so I could go and buy the prawns. I don't stock them. And when I got back I thought it would be better if I just stayed closed.'

'But what about your customers?'

'I doubt very much they'll have noticed. Business next door is very slow these days.'

It was such a shame — his shop was a useful general store, but the locals seemed to be more drawn to the out-of-town supermarket.

She shook her head. 'You'll lose even more customers if you keep closing up on a whim.'

He took her hand and looked down into her eyes. And, for a moment, she forgot to breathe.

'I wanted to shut the shop and make the cake, so I did.'

His gaze was steady — daring her to argue — but the gentle touch of his hands holding hers was what melted her heart in the end.

'Thank you, Angus,' she told him seriously. That he had taken time out of his working day to make a birthday cake for Teddy, when she knew he thought it was daft meant the world to her. 'I appreciate it.'

He gave a short nod and abruptly let go of her hand and walked to the door.

'I'll be back in a minute.'

She stared after him as he left the café and wondered if maybe she had lectured him too much about unscheduled shop closures.

Had she offended him?

She'd only been worried because she knew his shop was often bereft of customers — but really she should have kept her views to herself. He'd been running his own business for years.

She wondered if she should run after him and apologise.

Just as she made up her mind that she should, there was a gentle tap on the glass of the large window at the front of the café. Fourteen pairs of eyes — one pair human, the rest feline — turned to investigate.

Maxine pushed the blinds aside and made out a familiar figure in the shadows outside the window. She hurried to let him back in.

'I didn't just make a cake for Teddy,'

he confessed as he held a cake box aloft.

'Meow,' Gladys said hopefully, as she leapt onto his shoulder.

'Sorry, Gladys — not for you.' He smiled at Maxine as he handed the box over. 'Happy Birthday.'

She lifted the lid and found another cat cake — but this one was in the shape of a cat rather than being made of cat-friendly food — a black and white cat with a sparkle in her eyes, much like Gladys.

'It's sponge cake,' he told her. 'No tuna in sight with that one.'

'I can't believe you made this for me,' she said, grinning up at him. 'It's gorgeous. Thank you.' She stood on tiptoe and brushed her lips against his.

'I'm a man of many talents.' He laughed — but Maxine knew, despite his jokey tone, that what he said was true. Whatever he turned his hand to, he seemed to excel at.

'How are you at cake eating?' she asked.

'Town champion for the past three years.'

'Good, then maybe you can stay a while and help me eat some of this.'

Maybe, just as she'd insisted to Sabrina earlier, it was too soon to think of being in love. But there was nobody she'd rather sit and eat cake with on her birthday evening.

She might have told herself for years that she was way too old to bother with something like a birthday — but, nonetheless, she found there was something very enticing about the fact that Angus was making a fuss over her.

9

Hogmanay at the Cat Café

The weeks passed quickly, and autumn soon faded into winter.

Before Maxine knew where she was, the talk was of Christmas.

'Do you want to share lunch again this year?' she asked Angus one day while she was in his shop.

'I said I'd go and see my mum.' He paused. 'I'd rather spend it with you.'

She smiled. 'I'd rather you were with me, too, but if you've promised your mum . . . '

'You could come with me?'

Too soon. She and Angus were getting on well, but meeting his mother was maybe pushing things a bit too quickly.

'I'd better stay with the cats,' she said. And she could see by his smile that he knew she was making an excuse.

'I'll be back after Boxing Day,' he told her. 'And we'll have Hogmanay to look forward to. We could go to the party at the community centre. That's if you want to?'

The thought of Hogmanay kept her happy over the days that Angus was away. Sabrina invited her for Christmas lunch with her family, and that was nice, too. But even nicer was Angus's kiss of greeting when he came to the café to see her on his return.

And then, suddenly, they were all preparing for Hogmanay.

'I'll just nip next door to Angus's shop to fetch a few essentials,' she told Sabrina as she put on her outdoor shoes and headed for the door.

Angus was busy with a customer when she got there.

'My lights have gone out and my house is in darkness. It's only two o'clock in the afternoon. What will it be like once the sun goes down?' Mrs Watkins was monopolising his attention at the counter as Maxine walked into the shop and headed for the stack of baskets by the till. 'I was vacuuming when it happened — I can't even finish cleaning my house.'

He found the time to glance over at Maxine and wink discreetly in her direction. She smiled in response.

'It's probably a fuse, Mrs Watkins,' he said.

Maxine grabbed a basket and went to pick up the few bits and pieces she needed to see her through the next couple of days, when Angus's shop would be shut.

'I really don't know what I'm going to do,' Mrs Watkins continued. 'My family are travelling from Edinburgh; they'll be here any minute. How am I supposed to entertain them if I've no electricity? And what electrician would come out at this time on Hogmanay?'

Maxine had no doubt that Angus would step in to help. The question was if he would take this strong hint, or if he would wait until Mrs Watkins asked straight out for a favour. At one time she had no doubt he would have taken the latter option, but recently his gruff exterior had softened quite considerably.

'Do you want me to pop around to take a look?'

He didn't disappoint, and Maxine smiled again as she put some milk and bread into her basket.

'Would you do that, Angus? That would be lovely of you — if you're sure you don't mind.' Mrs Watkins sounded both surprised and delighted — almost as though she hadn't quite realised that Angus had been an electrician before he'd taken over the shop.

'I'll be closing up early today, so I'll see you in the next half hour or so.'

Mrs Watkins gave a little wave as she made her way out of the shop.

'What?' Angus demanded as Maxine approached the till still grinning.

'You're just a big softie,' she accused.

'Maybe.' He smiled, holding her gaze. 'But I may need to go back to electrical work one of these days, so it's as well to keep my hand in.'

'Did she even buy anything when she was here?'

He shook his head. 'And that's part of the reason I might need to go back to electrical work . . . '

Maxine knew he was struggling with the shop — and she was grateful he had the option to return to his former career. But on a personal level, she liked to know he was here, next door to her café.

'I'll miss you if you do wind up the business.'

That earned her another grin. 'For the moment, I'm just helping out someone with a fuse box problem.'

'Just as long as you're back in time for the party tonight.' Maxine had been looking forward to seeing in the New Year with Angus ever since they'd arranged to go to go to the community centre for the bells — even if it would be along with almost everyone else in town.

'I'll pick you up at ten, as arranged.'

'Come around at nine. We can have a drink before we head over.'

The opportunity to spend time alone before the party was too much to resist.

★   ★   ★

When Maxine got back to the cat café, Sabrina was thumping a cushion. 'There,' she said with a tone of satisfaction as she placed it back on the sofa, 'all ready for Gladys to flatten again when the whim takes her.'

Maxine smiled, glancing around for the feline culprit.

That was the thing with having so many cats around — however hard you worked, things were never tidy for very long.

At the moment, however, Gladys was too busy to bother flattening any cushions, having moved to admire her own reflection in a bauble that was hanging from the tree that Angus had again this year managed to attach to the wall. Christmas trees attached to walls were necessities when there were so many cats. Maxine had discovered that the hard way.

'She's going to go for that bauble in a minute.' Sabrina wasn't making a psychic prediction — more an observation based on her extensive knowledge of cat behaviour.

Maxine wasn't surprised when Gladys leapt up and swiped the decoration off the tree with one large paw. The bauble shot across the room — luckily it was made of plastic, so there was no harm done — and a scatter of Gladys's adopted feline siblings raced after it.

Maxine laughed. 'Never a dull moment here.'

'We need to take the tree down now Christmas is over,' Sabrina said. 'Before they do any real damage. I'm surprised they've left it alone as long as they have.'

'We'll take it down next week, once all the fuss of the New Year has died down. The customers expect some sort of tree.'

If she was honest, customers or not,

Maxine wasn't in too much of a hurry to be rid of the tree. With snow dusting the windows and the ground outside, the tree and the fairy lights made the place very cosy this Hogmanay afternoon.

'Why don't you get off home,' she suggested to Sabrina. 'Take your time and get ready for the party tonight.'

They had only taken bookings for the morning and early afternoon sessions today, so that they could close early and prepare for tonight's planned festivities. There really was no point in Sabrina hanging around.

Sabrina didn't need telling twice. 'Well, if you're sure . . . ' She grinned as she headed for the coat cupboard. 'Will you be going along to the party with Angus?'

Maxine nodded. 'He's going to pop by later and we'll walk across together.'

The hall was only across the green from the café, but last year she hadn't gone, preferring instead to spend a quiet night in with her cats. This year, though, her cats were truly settled, and she was confident they would be fine for a few hours. And this year, there was someone special she wanted to see in the New Year in with . . .

'Ed said they've planned a big surprise at midnight for everyone.' Sabrina smiled as she mentioned her husband. He'd been working on the committee that had arranged the party for the town.

'Can't wait to see what it is.' Maxine smiled.

'Me neither. I've been trying to get him to tell me, but he says I'll find out soon enough. It's really annoying — he's normally rubbish at keeping secrets.'

Maxine laughed. Ed was the sweetest man ever, and she knew that he would only be keeping quiet now so that Sabrina would enjoy the surprise when it was revealed.

'I'm hoping they've got a live ceilidh band,' Sabrina said as she headed for the door. 'Those records are OK, but it would be nice to dance to some live music. I'll let you know if I manage to get him to spill the beans.'

And with that, she was away.

It didn't take long. Maxine had barely settled, with a cat or two on her lap, when her mobile rang.

'It's fireworks,' Sabrina said, her tone indicating she wasn't best pleased. 'That's the surprise.'

Maxine sat up, immediately alert. Teddy looked disgusted and leapt from her lap to the safely of the floor. 'How can they plan fireworks without telling anyone?'

At least on bonfire night fireworks had been a given, and people had been able to plan for the safety and comfort of their pets.

She could almost hear Sabrina rolling her eyes with exasperation. 'That's exactly what I said. Ed thinks it's OK because they've done a risk assessment — and he says everyone will be expecting fireworks on New Year's Eve.'

Maxine thought back to the peaceful Hogmanay exactly a year ago. Maybe, in some places, they might have expected a pyrotechnic display, but not here.

'I'm sure they meant well,' she said, trying to be kind, 'but it would have been nice to have had some notice.' She made a mental note to spread the word to those who needed to know. A surprise was one thing, but not at the expense of the wellbeing of the animal population.

'It's only a small display.' Sabrina's tone was almost apologetic now. 'They didn't raise the money for anything spectacular. It probably won't last longer than five minutes. But they're setting it up in Bill Appleton's garden — behind the community centre — so it lights up the sky above.'

The same sky that was across the green from Maxine's cats. Even though her windows were double glazed and her cats were pretty relaxed, New Year fireworks would no doubt be loud — and animals could be easily terrified. She wouldn't risk leaving her cats alone tonight.

Quickly she found her mobile and called Angus's number. It went straight to answerphone. 'He's helping Mrs Watkins,' she told Gladys as she listened to his pre-recorded message.

As expected, Gladys didn't reply; she sat and watched Maxine's attempts to contact Angus with indifferent feline eyes.

The beep sounded and Maxine took a deep breath. She hated leaving a message on these things, but needs must.

'Angus, it's Maxine. About tonight — I've only just found out there will be fireworks. I can't go to the party. I mean I could pop in for a little while, before the display, but I'd need to be home by midnight because of my cats, so it doesn't seem worth it. So I'm sorry, but I have to cancel.'

She sighed again before disconnecting the call, knowing she had been babbling and only hoping he would be able to make out the gist her message.

'Well,' she told the supervising Gladys, 'that could have gone better.'

'Mew,' Gladys vocalised her agreement, before walking off to challenge Sadie's claim over the catnip ball.

Next time, Maxine thought, she'd rehearse her message; maybe even write it down. Or maybe she would wait until he was free and pop round to see him.

'Meow.' The cry brought her back to the present and she found the Bengal brothers, Alfie and Sam, standing hopefully by the kitchen door.

'Time for tea,' she told them with a smile, and the eleven other cats all joined the duo to wait it out by the door as Maxine went to prepare their meals.

OK, so she was disappointed that she wouldn't be able to go out tonight. But she didn't begrudge a second of the time she would be spending with her cats.

★ ★ ★

Angus didn't call her back.

Not that she was surprised — what

175

was there really for him to say? He knew her well enough to know that, with the prospect of so much noise, she would have to stay at home with her cats no matter what he said. So really there was no point in him trying to persuade her.

With a sigh, she settled down for the wait until midnight, with the company of a good book.

Moments later, Sadie leapt onto her lap. Not to be outdone, Gladys climbed onto her shoulder.

'You're getting too big for that, my darling,' she said. Gladys, seeming to understand, shifted most of her weight onto the back of the chair. 'It's a pity Angus isn't here, isn't it? His shoulder's broad enough for you to sit on comfortably.'

That was the reason she was missing Angus this evening — as a convenient chair for Gladys. Wishing he was here had nothing to do with missing his company — or the ready laugh that was infectious, the dark eyes that seemed to burn into her soul, the kisses that made her heart sing . . .

But she did wonder if Angus would find someone else to kiss when the bells struck midnight.

★ ★ ★

She was so engrossed in solving the murder mystery between the pages of her book that when a knock sounded on the café window, she nearly jumped out of her skin. Before she could react, there was another knock. Then another.

One by one, the cats moved into hiding, disturbed by the noise.

'Happy New Year!' The merry shouting and cheering were several hours premature, but it sounded as though the group outside had already been celebrating.

Annoyed, Maxine put her book to one side and pulled the blinds open. The shadowy figures on the pavement cheered.

Furious now, Maxine went to the

storm porch before throwing back the bolts, intent on giving these raucous well-wishers a piece of her mind.

'Hey, you lot.' She recognised Angus's authoritative tone as she opened door. 'What are you playing at? There are cats in there — do you want to frighten them to death?'

Maxine saw horror dawn onto the faces of the four lads outside.

'Sorry.' The boy closest to Maxine had a sheepish look about him. 'We didn't think. We saw your lights on and just wanted to wish you a happy New Year.'

It seemed that good intentions rather than malice had been behind the noise. Maxine relaxed a little — the harsh words that were ready on her tongue remained unsaid.

'Just be more thoughtful in future,' Angus warned.

Maxine stood aside to let him in, a bottle of something bubbly under his arm, and she closed the door.

'How did you get on with Mrs Watkins?'

He grinned. 'All sorted. She was able to greet her family in a freshly vacuumed house — with lights on.'

'Are you on your way to the party?' she asked.

'I was planning to go. I got ready and everything.' He nodded down at his outfit and she smiled. He looked good in a kilt — he had the legs for it. 'But then I saw I had a message . . . Sorry I didn't spot it earlier.'

'I'm sorry for the late notice, but I really can't leave them. They got enough of a fright with those boys knocking at the window. I can't imagine what they'll be like when the fireworks go off if I'm not here to soothe them.'

He gave a nod. 'I can't believe the committee thought fireworks would be a suitable surprise for somewhere as quiet as this town. We're not used to that much noise around here.'

She smiled. 'You'd better get going if you're not going to miss all the fun.'

He frowned. 'I had kind of hoped you'd let me stay here, with you and the cats. I brought this.' He held out the bottle. 'I thought we could toast the New Year.'

'But you said you wanted to go to the party . . . '

'What I actually said was that I wanted to see the New Year in with you,' he reminded her softly, drawing her closer. And, even though it wasn't even nearly midnight yet, he kissed her anyway.

★   ★   ★

It took them a while, but when the cats realised that any possible danger from the window knocking had passed, they came out of hiding.

Gladys made a beeline for Angus and had a huge fuss made of her before she wandered off to nap next to the radiator.

All seemed right with the world. Maxine put soft music on to soothe the cats after their fright — and to hopefully mask any new outburst outside — and she and Angus were dancing, her head on his shoulder, while they waited for midnight.

When her mobile burst to life on the counter, she stopped mid-step, startled.

'Maxine, it's me — Sabrina. I'm outside. Ed and Chloe are with me. Will you let us in?'

'What are you doing here?' she asked, as the family brought the bitter chill of a snowy Hogmanay indoors with them.

'We thought you might need some extra cat-minding tonight.' Ed gave an embarrassed smile. 'I'm so sorry, Maxine — I can't believe I didn't think that the fireworks would affect the cats.'

Maxine knew it wouldn't have been deliberate. 'You were trying to do a nice thing for the town,' she said. 'But what are you doing here? Won't they miss you at the party? After all, you helped arrange it.'

He shook his head. 'Nah, they won't miss me.'

'And you're not supposed to be working tonight,' she reminded Sabrina.

'Doesn't that say a lot about how

much I love my job if I'd rather be here cuddling cats, making them feel secure, rather than living it up in the community centre?'

'Oh, please let us stay?' Chloe chipped in. 'We'd much rather be here — and the cats might need us.'

The first burst of noisy fireworks heralded the New Year — they'd been so busy arguing over who was to stay that they'd missed it.

'Looks like it's settled and you're staying,' Angus told them as another loud burst from outside had cats scattering in all directions. They wanted to hide, that was obvious; to snuggle together into corners and cubbyholes where they felt safest. But the people they loved most would be here for them when they emerged and needed to be comforted.

'I think it's over,' Maxine dared to say as the alarming explosions stopped as suddenly as they had begun. Sabrina had been right — the display hadn't taken long.

'Are the cats OK?' Chloe peered around, trying to spot them.

Sadie was the first cat to emerge. She bravely popped her nose, then a hairy paw, out from her hiding place behind the counter. Then, one by one, the others cautiously appeared.

'It's quarter past midnight,' Angus said, glancing at the clock on the wall and barely flinching as Gladys took a flying leap onto his shoulder, despite the fact she landed with a force that would have felled a lesser man. 'A bit late, but what do you say we toast the New Year? There's champagne for those who want it — and I'm sure Maxine can find some orange juice for Chloe.'

They all raised their glasses. 'Happy New Year.'

When Maxine had moved here, she had been alone in the world — and it hadn't mattered because she'd been intent on starting her new life as an independent businesswoman.

Somehow, along the way, she had acquired a family of sorts — her cats and these friends who she hadn't even known that long, but who she loved with all her heart. People she could rely on, even when it meant they had to forgo the fun evening they had planned to sit in and help with her cats.

'We should go back to the party,' Sabrina said apologetically. 'Come with us?'

Maxine shook her head. 'The cats seem OK, but I just want to make sure; it's been an exciting night for them. But I can't thank you guys enough for being here.'

There were New Year hugs before they went. And then there was just her and Angus . . .

'You not going with them?' she asked, even though she'd firmly closed the door.

He got to his feet, took her hands and drew her closer. 'Without you? Not a chance.'

And, finally, the moment Maxine had been waiting for, as Angus's lips met hers for her first kiss of this New Year.

10

Maxine's Man

'The show starts at eight,' Angus told Maxine, leaning casually against the counter with arms folded neatly — almost as though the giant Norwegian forest cat on his shoulder weighed nothing at all. 'I thought I could close the shop early and we could get away as soon as you finish up here. Then we might have time for a quick bite to eat beforehand.'

Maxine liked the sound of that. This was to be their first night out of the New Year, and she'd been looking forward to it. Angus had booked tickets to see her favourite comedian, and a meal would start the evening perfectly. 'Maybe we could eat at the little bistro across the road from the theatre?'

'I'll book a table.' He grinned. 'I'd best get back to the shop, but I'll pop back at half five to collect you.'

Maxine frowned. She didn't close the café until five, and she'd need to shower and get changed from her uniform of jeans and T-shirt into something a little smarter. And do her make-up . . .

'Take this,' she said, rummaging in the drawer under the till and emerging with a key to the café's back door. 'You can let yourself in and make yourself a cup of tea so I don't have to interrupt my getting ready time by answering the door.' She put the key into his upturned palm.

It seemed so much more than just a key for convenience. It was a significant step in their relationship. By giving him key, she was trusting him with her café. With her cats.

The way Angus was maintaining eye contact, with a solemn expression on his face, confirmed he understood the significance.

'You're sure?' His hand was still outstretched, almost as though he was offering her the chance to snatch the key back if she wanted to change her mind.

But she'd never been surer of anything in her life. 'You might as well hang on to it afterwards,' she said, smiling. 'You never know when I might be glad of a neighbour with a spare key.'

But they both knew it meant more than that.

He grinned and slipped the key into his pocket and turned his attention to Gladys, who was still perched on his shoulder. 'OK, trouble.' He lifted the cat and set her down on the counter.

'Mew,' Gladys complained, and Angus ruffled the fur behind her ear.

'I'll see you later.' Then he turned to Maxine, and even though the wink was barely there, she noticed it.

Her heart fluttered.

Angus let himself out through the storm porch at the front of the café just as Sabrina, the café assistant, arrived for work.

★ ★ ★

187

Maxine always left the window blinds closed when they were getting the café ready for opening. It wouldn't do to let the guests see the hard work behind keeping the place spick and span — it would ruin the magic.

When everything was as it should be, Maxine threw open the blinds, allowing the visitors their first glimpse of the cats.

As always, there was much excitement. They nudged each other, they pointed at a cat here, smiled at a fury face there . . . And thirteen cats stared back at them in a leisurely fashion.

She never tired of this. Sensing the growing anticipation of the crowd waiting to be let in — some of them regular visitors, too — validated the decision she'd made to give up her career to open this place.

She made people happy. And that had to be one of the most important jobs of all.

As she glanced along the queue, someone caught her eye — a man lurking at the back of the line, looking for all the world as though he was about to meet his doom. He didn't look a part of the joyous crowd outside. He didn't fit in with them at all.

Maybe a doting dad who had given in to nagging and reluctantly brought his offspring? Or a hesitant boyfriend? She'd seen plenty of both types of visitors — and both sorts were generally won round by the end of the session. But there was something about this man . . .

She frowned. He seemed oddly familiar. There was something about the close cut of his hair, the way his shoulders hunched up against the cold . . .

Then it hit her as suddenly as though a bolt of lightning had struck through the café.

'What's wrong?' Sabrina was looking on with a worried frown. 'You look like you've seen a ghost.'

Maxine made a monumental effort to pull herself together. 'Robert,' she managed to croak. 'It's Robert.'

'Robert? Your ex-fiancé?' Sabrina

followed Maxine's gaze to the window. 'Outside?'

Maxine nodded. Out of context, she hadn't recognised him — and for that she felt supremely daft. She'd been engaged to him for two years.

'Looks like he's waiting to come in.' Maxine frantically tried to remember if he was on the guest list. 'I don't recall seeing his name when I checked the bookings first thing.' For one wild moment, Maxine considered sending him away, giving him the excuse that there wasn't a table for him.

'I took a booking from a man just after I arrived this morning,' Sabrina admitted, turning pale. 'I didn't catch his name and I didn't like to keep asking. I put him in as John Doe.'

And Maxine hadn't noticed the code for an unknown man. She bit her lip. She really didn't want to see him. He was firmly in her past and had no place in the bright future she'd made for herself.

But if he'd made a booking, she had

no option . . . Maxine wasn't in the habit of turning people away when they'd booked.

She glanced again towards the window. 'I wasn't expecting to ever see him again.'

Maybe she could escape the back way. But that would leave Sabrina on her own, and even though she was more than capable, it wasn't really fair to leave her with a full house.

'Correct me if I'm wrong,' Sabrina said, craning her neck for a better view of their impending visitor, 'but isn't Robert the ex-fiancé who doesn't like cats?'

Maxine nodded. His distaste for cats had been the final straw for their relationship. They'd both unhappy for a while by that point. They had been aiming for different goals. As accountants, they'd worked hard to gain their qualifications. But while Robert had seen his future in numbers and balance sheets, Maxine's heart hadn't been in it. She'd wanted to start a business of her own.

When Robert had laughed at her dream of opening a cat café, she'd known it was over between them.

'What on earth is he doing here if he doesn't like cats?' Sabrina seemed as perplexed as Maxine.

She was going to have to let him in. The queue was growing restless, and it was already a few minutes past the start of their session.

She pasted on a smile as she headed for the door. 'Only one way to find out . . . '

★   ★   ★

As the other guests played with and cooed over the cats, Robert sat ramrod-straight in a corner chair and looked more miserable than Maxine had ever seen him before. Which was saying something, because Robert had made something of a hobby out of being displeased.

Maxine wondered now why she hadn't broken their engagement sooner. He'd often made her displeased, too.

Though maybe she hadn't realised that until recently. When she thought of how being in Angus's company made her heart soar, she thanked goodness she'd discovered in time just how unsuited she and Robert really had been.

If they'd married . . . She tried not to shudder at the thought.

She took a deep breath. 'Hello, Robert.'

He looked up from his chair and frowned. 'I can't believe this place.'

Maxine smiled. 'It is rather special, isn't it.' She deliberately misunderstood his statement. She knew she should probably ask him what he wanted, but the words wouldn't form. Instead, she went into her default café owner mode. 'What would you like to drink?' she asked with perfect politeness, preparing to write his order down in her little book.

He wrinkled his nose. 'I can't believe you actually serve refreshments in this place. What about cat hairs? What about germs?'

Once, a very long time ago, she had

found his fastidiousness oddly charming. Now it just irritated her. 'We keep the place clean,' she told him haughtily. 'And the kitchen is a cat-free environment, in any case.'

He didn't look convinced.

'The place has been inspected. I have food hygiene certificates.'

None of it seemed to register with Robert.

'You can't come to a cat café and neither interact with the animals, nor have anything to eat or drink. You might as well not have bothered.'

She knew she sounded sharp, but really, what did he expect? He was going to infect the whole session with his misery if he wasn't careful. Maxine's Cat Café was a happy place — there was no place for Robert's special kind of grumpiness.

'Oh, OK,' he said grudgingly. 'If you insist, I'll have a cup of tea. Two sugars and no milk.'

She raised an eyebrow. He'd always liked his tea very milky.

'Milk will make it harder to see if there are any cat hairs floating in my cup.'

She gave a quick nod and bit her tongue to stop herself form replying.

When she came back with his tea, he was staring suspiciously at Teddy, who was sitting on the floor a few feet away. 'What's wrong with that cat?'

'What do you mean?' She put Robert's tea on a nearby table.

'It keeps looking at me.'

'You're in his chair.'

Robert looked startled. 'His chair? You can't possibly expect me to get up for an animal.'

Maxine sighed. 'Normally, if his chair's occupied, he would have no problem sitting on a lap.'

Robert shuddered visibly and Maxine could see exactly why Teddy wasn't going near him. Cats could sense when they were disliked.

His eyes narrowed as he peered suspiciously at Teddy. 'What have you done to him?'

'What do you mean?'

'Well, he's all . . . ' Robert waved a hand towards Teddy's unblinking face. 'He's all curly.'

'He's a Selkirk Rex.'

The blank look she received in response showed that Robert was unfamiliar with that breed. 'Did you perm him or something?'

'What are you talking about?'

'Those curls can't be natural. Have you had his fur in curlers?'

If she had needed proof that Robert knew nothing about cats, this was it. 'No. The curls are entirely natural.' She spoke slowly to ensure that the message got across. 'That's how he was born. I wouldn't put a cat's fur in curlers — they wouldn't like it and it would be cruel.'

Teddy was looking hurt. She wasn't sure he understood the words, but there was no getting away from the fact that he was aware he was being spoken about in derogatory terms.

She felt a pang of anger towards

Robert. She knew he wasn't fond of cats, but how dare he make one of her babies feel so uncomfortable? And in his own home, too.

'Why exactly are you here, Robert? It's pretty obvious you're not here for the cats.'

'No,' he said. 'I'm here for you.'

Maxine felt her eyebrows rise to her hairline. 'That sounds alarming to say the least.'

'I need to talk to you.'

That was as may be, but Maxine wasn't that keen on talking to him.

'I'm afraid I really don't have time to chat.' She waved an arm around the café. 'As you can see, I've a full café.'

'Surely you can spare five minutes?'

Despite her reluctance to have anything to do with him, she had to admit that a part of her was curious about why he was here. 'Is there something wrong?'

He shook his head. 'Not wrong — but it's important that we talk.'

'Come back after closing time,' she

decided reluctantly. 'But I'll only be able to spare you five minutes. I'm going out tonight.'

With a red-hot date to look forward to, she wasn't going to keep Angus waiting for anyone.

★   ★   ★

'That ex of yours is outside again,' Sabrina practically whispered, almost as though he might be able to hear her through the double glazing as she closed the blinds for the night.

'He wants to talk.' Maxine frowned. 'I told him to come back after closing time.' She was wondering now if she should have told him to come back tomorrow — she didn't want to put herself in a bad mood before Angus came to pick her up.

'But I thought you and Angus were going to see that comedian?'

'We are. Robert won't be staying long.' Five minutes, she had told him, and that was exactly what she'd meant.

'Do you want me to hang around?'

Maxine shook her head. 'No, it's fine, thanks. I just need to find out what he wants. It wasn't appropriate to talk earlier, not with everyone here.'

Sabrina hesitated by the coat cupboard. 'I can hang on for five minutes. Make sure he doesn't cause any trouble.'

Again, Maxine shook her head. 'You get going. You need to collect Chloe from her art club, remember? I'll be fine.'

Sabrina let Robert into the café on her way out.

'They're still here.' He glanced around nervously as thirteen pairs of feline eyes regarded him with equal suspicion. 'I didn't think they'd still be here.'

'Where on earth did you think they'd be, Robert? They live here.'

He shrugged, looking uncomfortable as he sat down at the nearest table.

Maxine didn't offer him a drink. She didn't want to give him the chance to call into question her café's hygiene credentials for a second time. Besides, with one eye on the clock, she knew there wasn't much time.

'Now, how can I help you?'

He cleared his throat, gave the cats one last suspicious glance, then began to speak.

'I've been made a partner of the firm.' He put the information out there, and sat back smugly, waiting to be congratulated.

Maxine couldn't see why he'd bothered to seek her out to share this news, but she knew that to Robert this would mean as much as the café did to her. She found it in her heart to be pleased for him.

'That's good news. Congratulations.'

'I knew you'd be pleased.' He lifted his head and puffed out his chest. 'It means we can get married straight away, and put all this nonsense — ' He paused to look haughtily around Maxine's cats. ' — behind us.'

Propelled by shock, Maxine sat down, even though she needed to start getting ready and didn't have time for such luxuries.

'I'm sorry?'

'The other partners are all married,' he explained, putting his proposal into the least romantic terms that Maxine could have ever imagined. 'It would be useful, for dinners and things, if I was, too.'

Maxine sighed. He was suggesting a marriage of convenience. She had never felt less flattered in her life.

'We can go ahead and arrange that big wedding my mother always said we should wait until we could afford.'

She'd liked Robert's mother — she would have been a good mother-in-law. But getting married because the groom needed a convenient wife to attend work functions had to go down in history as the worst reason ever.

'But we're not engaged anymore.'

He waved that objection away. 'Easily remedied.' With a flourish, he pulled an engagement ring from his pocket.

Unless she was very much mistaken,

it was the very ring she had handed back to him in another lifetime.

He grabbed her hand and slid the ring onto her finger.

'There, back where it belongs.' He smiled, satisfied with a job well done. 'Now you have no reason not to leave this place and come back with me to where you belong.'

As Maxine was rendered mute by indignation, she noticed a movement from the corner of her eye. Angus was taking in the scene from near the kitchen door. He must have let himself in through the back door, just as Maxine had told him to.

Her overriding awareness was of the look of shock on his face — something her own would mirror, she was sure.

'Meow,' Gladys, delighted to have noticed her favourite human, broke the silence.

A mask of neutrality descended over Angus's features. 'I see I've arrived at an awkward time,' he said.

If the situation hadn't been so

absurd, Maxine would have laughed. But all she could do was watch with mounting horror as Angus momentarily fussed over Gladys before he turned and left just as silently as he'd arrived.

'Who was that?' Robert asked.

Recovering her wits, Maxine slipped the ring off and handed it back to Robert for a second time.

'That was my boyfriend,' she told him, realising this was the first time she'd described Angus as such. 'Here, take this ring back, please. I can't marry you. And, if you're honest, you don't really want to marry me, either.'

'How can you possibly say that?'

'Because it's true. If you did, then you wouldn't have used work as an excuse.'

'But . . .'

'You haven't tried to make contact. Not once since I left.' She sighed. She didn't want to hurt him, but she had to make him see the truth. 'Besides, you haven't mentioned love in all of this.'

'Surely that's a given.'

She shook her head. 'If you really loved me you would accept my cats, rather than expecting me to abandon them.'

'Don't be silly, Maxine. Who in their right mind would want to live with all these animals?'

'Me.' She showed him to the door, intent on taking no more nonsense. 'If you loved me as a bride deserves to be loved, you would learn to love my cats. If only because they matter to me.'

There was someone who had done exactly that, and she would never settle for less. And now she was going to have to go and find him and explain the situation he had walked in on.

Because she very much feared he had misunderstood.

★   ★   ★

'I'll have to go in my jeans,' Maxine said apologetically when Angus came to the door and let her in. 'As you saw, I was held up by a visitor.'

'You look fine in jeans,' he said gruffly. 'So, your man's in town.' He didn't look thrilled, Maxine was pleased to note. If the roles had been reversed and it had been Angus's ex-wife who had happened by with suggestions of marriage, she would have been equally miffed.

'Yes,' she told him, keeping eye contact and trying not to smile. 'He is.'

But when she saw his shoulders deflate and hurt fill his eyes, she couldn't keep the teasing up. 'It's you, you daft thing.' She nudged his arm. 'I rather thought *you* were my man.'

And there it was, the grin that she loved so much — the one that made her breath and her heart flutter. 'That is,' she added almost shyly, 'if you want to be.'

When he pulled her closer and kissed her thoroughly, he left no doubt that he most definitely did.

11

Escape

Maxine perched on a stool behind the counter of her cat café, a concerned frown on her face.

'What do you mean you're closing the shop for the day?' She knew Angus's grocer's shop next door was none of her business, but she couldn't help being worried.

By any measure, Angus's business was struggling. He would be the first to admit that. Closing up on a whim at such short notice wasn't likely to help matters.

Angus didn't seem to share Maxine's anxiety over the situation. He leaned casually against the counter, wearing jeans, T-shirt, and an easy grin as he fended off cats in all directions. 'I feel like taking the day off.'

Gladys and Sadie, not about to be deterred by his efforts, were vying for space on the same broad shoulder.

'There isn't enough room on Angus's shoulder for two,' Maxine said, still frowning as she gently lifted Sadie into her arms. But the cats weren't the problem.

'Your customers, Angus . . . '

'Are very few and far between.' Careful not to dislodge Gladys from her spot, he reached out and took Maxine's hand and held it tight. 'I know what you're thinking — and you're right — but it's a nice day. I thought I'd take a drive up north and maybe visit my mother.'

An admirable motive, but still . . . Given his current cashflow predicament, closing up for the day was the last thing he should be doing.

But he was right, it was a nice day. And he worked hard. He deserved a day off.

She sighed. Surely there had to be some way to help him.

Angus had been good to her and to her cats, taking any opportunity he could to help with the cat café. Now it was time to pay him back for some of those kindnesses.

'Mondays are always quieter here at the café. I can easily handle the bookings and any casual drop-ins on my own.' She smiled, knowing she'd hit on the perfect solution. 'Once Sabrina gets here, why don't I send her to take care of the shop for you?'

'Funny you should say that. I had been about to ask how you'd think Sabrina would manage here at the café on her own. I'd rather hoped you'd come with me.'

He gave her hand a squeeze, and she was suddenly unable to form a coherent argument as one thought consumed her.

'I . . . I . . . ' At an uncharacteristic loss for words, she stared at him as he lifted her hand and grazed her fingers with his lips.

'Escape with me for the day,' he urged.

She gulped in a lungful of air. 'You want me to meet you mother?'

This was more than a day out he was proposing. This was the next big step in their relationship, and it was a big deal.

'It's about time, don't you think?'

They had been dating a while, it was true, but she hadn't expected to have this surprise sprung on her.

'This is rather sudden, Angus.' Though in all honesty, if she'd been given notice she would have only had more time to worry.

Maxine had never been a coward. She liked to face any situation head on. But this was Angus's mother they were talking about. And it wasn't that she objected to meeting anyone's mother in principle — she tended to get along well with all sorts of mothers — but Angus meant a lot to her. What if his mother didn't like her?

'She doesn't bite.'

'I'm sure she doesn't.' Though Maxine was really sure of no such thing. She'd seen a photo of Elizabeth

McRae in Angus's flat, and the woman's angry frown in that snap had been terrifying. Not to mention the tiny detail that Angus had already told her that his mum was more a dog person and had little time for cats.

What could they possibly have in common?

'You're going to have to meet her eventually.'

Maxine sighed. 'I know. But today? Are you sure this is what you want, Angus?'

'Yes, it is.' He stood up straight and lifted Gladys down onto the counter, ruffling the fur behind the cat's ears and earning himself an adoring purr for his troubles. 'Besides, she wants to meet you.'

Maxine felt her face flush. 'Your mother knows about me?' That made things a little better, knowing that she wasn't going to turn up like a nasty surprise on the doorstep of a woman who was blissfully unaware she existed.

'I may have mentioned you once or

twice. In passing.'

He was making it sound casual, but Maxine knew what a big deal this was. They had been very much downplaying their romance. Angus was wary of giving his heart to anyone after his particularly unpleasant divorce. It had taken Maxine a long time to break through his defences and to get him to even go on a date. And there were days she was still not sure he was completely over his experience.

But the fact he had mentioned Maxine to his mother proved more than anything that he was ready to move on. That he wanted their relationship to work. If Angus could do that, then surely Maxine could be brave and face up to this meeting.

She glanced around the café. Thirteen pairs of eyes looked back. She didn't like to leave them, but her feline family would be fine with Sabrina for the day, she was sure. Her assistant was more than capable. She wouldn't even be considering gallivanting off if she had even a sliver of doubt.

'I'll even buy you a nice lunch while we're about it.' It was almost as though Angus could sense her weakening resolve as he played his ace card.

She smiled. 'Well, if there's lunch involved then how can I refuse?'

*   *   *

'You look nice,' Sabrina said as Maxine walked back into the café half an hour later.

She glanced down at her outfit. She'd chosen a floral dress in varying shades of blue and black, with a matching cardigan. The colours and pattern were just the right shade and design to disguise any rogue cat hairs that might turn up on her outfit.

Making the right impression was important.

'I thought I'd better make a bit of an effort. I didn't think Angus's mum would appreciate me turning up in my work clothes.'

Personally, she was rather fond of her jeans and cat café T-shirt, but she'd thought it might be nice to make an effort. For Angus's sake. And, despite telling herself sternly that there was nothing to be nervous about, she was still keen to make the right first impression.

Something of what she was feeling must have shown on her face, because Sabrina came over and gave her a quick hug.

'The cats will be fine,' she said, her tone reassuring, but misunderstanding Maxine's worries. 'I'll take good care of them.'

'I know you will.'

'And Chloe will jump at the chance of helping out after school,' Sabrina added.

Maxine smiled. Chloe, Sabrina's teenage daughter, was as passionate about the cats as Maxine was herself. She gave a quick nod.

'Just go and have a good time,' Sabrina urged, ushering her towards the door as Angus appeared at the window and gave a wave.

'I'll try.' Though as she made her way to the porch, every single cat in the café seemed determined to hamper her progress by getting deliberately under her feet.

'They know I'm leaving them,' she said as she nearly broke her neck tripping over both Teddy and Brian. 'They're trying to stop me going.'

Guilt at putting her cats through this turmoil momentarily vied with trepidation at the imminent meeting. It wasn't too late to make an excuse. Angus would understand . . .

But then Sabrina laughed, bringing Maxine to her senses. 'The cats can sense your anxiety, that's all. They just want to know that you're OK and they'll be fine once you're out of the door. Besides, you're not leaving them — you'll be back in a few hours.'

'That's true.' She sighed, hoping that by tonight she would be back here curled up with a cat or two on her lap and be wondering why she'd been so worried. 'Wish me luck.'

'What for? For meeting Angus's mother?' Sabrina looked surprised. 'You don't need luck. She's going to love you.'

Maxine wished she could believe that. 'But what if she doesn't? I'm terrified.' The words slipped out. She hadn't wanted to reveal so much, as seemed disloyal to Angus, but Sabrina was a good friend as well as the best assistant she could have hoped for.

'You're the bravest person I know. You walked out on a career that wasn't fulfilling, and on a man who made you unhappy, and you moved to a town where you knew nobody and started a successful business and made new friends. And you've found a man you're crazy about and who's just as crazy about you. Meeting his mum will be a breeze for someone like you.'

'Thanks.' With Sabrina's words ringing in her ears, Maxine could almost believe herself invincible.

'Ready?' Angus asked as Maxine

finally made it out onto the pavements.

'Yes.' Decisive. Certain. Confident. That was exactly the impression she wanted to give.

But then she risked a glance back towards the café to find Gladys and Sadie at the window, staring forlornly out at them. Gladys mouthed an inaudible meow that pulled at Maxine's heart.

Angus chuckled softly. 'I'd suggest bringing her,' he said, revealing he understood exactly how Maxine felt. 'But I don't think Cindy would react well.'

'Who's Cindy?'

'Mum's toy poodle.'

Maxine smiled, imagining a small dog would stand little chance against the bossy Norwegian forest cat. 'It's probably best for Cindy's sake that we leave Gladys at home.'

⋆　⋆　⋆

'I'm not really a dog person,' she warned Angus in the car as he told her about the little poodle that his mother doted on. 'I can't even pretend. Dogs scare me.'

He shook his head in disbelief. 'How can anyone not like dogs?'

'I don't dislike them, exactly.' She sighed. 'I was bitten by one when I was a child,' she admitted quietly. 'It wasn't serious, but I got a fright and I've avoided them ever since.'

'I suppose it's natural to be nervous of an animal that's given you a fright. If I'm honest, cats used to scare me.' He took the chance to glance across at her as they stopped at a red light.

Maxine was sceptical. The thought of this burly, gruff, and very capable man being scared of cats was unbelievable.

'Honestly, they did,' he insisted. 'You never know what a cat's thinking.'

'They're intelligent and have minds of their own, it's true.' The little scene her cats had put on when she'd left the café earlier more than proved that they were perfectly aware of what was going on. Not to mention the schemes and tricks they got up to day-to-day

— especially if there was food involved. 'What changed your mind?'

'A bundle of black and white fur named Gladys.' He threw her a quick grin.

'She loves you, too.' She smiled.

It wasn't only Glady who loved him. That had been proved without doubt today. Why else would she care so deeply about his mum liking her? And, given how keen he had been to bring her on this mission to meet the other woman in his life, she suspected her feelings might well be reciprocated. Though neither of them had actually said the words yet. And even though she was tempted to tell him now, she didn't want to frighten him by being the first to say it.

'And you'll learn to get on with Cindy, too, I'm sure.'

They were driving out of town now, and Maxine kept an eye on the passing scenery as they headed north.

'I hope you're right.' She sighed. Because she couldn't imagine making a worse impression than not getting on

218

with the hostess's pet. She knew how insulted she was when anyone showed her cats a cold shoulder.

Suddenly she was more worried about meeting the dog than she was about meeting his mother.

Maybe she would avoid Cindy. Maybe she would sit calmly and smile politely from a distance.

Yes, that seemed like the perfect strategy.

★   ★   ★

Maxine didn't get much of a chance to put that strategy into action.

As soon as they arrived, the front door to his mother's house opened, and a bundle of excited fur bounded out to them, barking noisily as she went. And Maxine was well and truly ambushed.

On instinct, she dropped to her knees and the little dog ran straight into her arms, licking her face, and accepting the fuss Maxine was suddenly making of her.

She heard Angus chuckle behind her. 'Scared of dogs, you say . . . Yes, I can see that.'

Laughing, she glanced up at him as Cindy continued with her warm welcome of happy barks and friendly licks.

'Maybe not entirely scared, after all,' she admitted, laughing as Cindy tried to lick her face. 'Maybe I just haven't met any of the right ones up close.'

'You've passed the first test, at least,' Angus said. At the sound of his voice, Cindy rushed to him. He scooped her up in one go. 'Cindy is very fussy about who she takes to.'

'She is, indeed,' a woman's voice said, and Maxine turned to see that Angus's mother had followed the dog out of the house. 'You must be Maxine. The cat woman I've heard so much about.'

Elizabeth McRae was barely into her sixties, and she was as tiny as her son was large, her hair as blonde as his was dark, but her frown was every bit as grumpy as his.

A family trait, Maxine thought as she tried not to be intimidated. The son's frown, after all, disguised the fact Angus was the loveliest man imaginable.

Gathering herself, Maxine got to her feet to offer a handshake.

'Tell me,' Elizabeth instructed sternly, taking Maxine's hand in a firm grip, 'what are your intentions towards my son?'

Maxine was a little startled and stared, not quite knowing how to reply. But then Angus threw back his head and laughed and she noticed the mischievous glint in Elizabeth's eyes. She realised she was being teased and she relaxed at once.

'I can see where Angus inherited his sense of humour from,' she said with a grin as they all went indoors, Cindy at their heels.

'So,' Elizabeth said once they were settled with cups of tea, 'cats. I hear you have a number. Tell me about them. And about your café.'

Maxine didn't need to be asked

twice. Let loose on her favourite subject, she could talk all day — and she quickly forgot to be worried about making any kind of impression.

For all that Elizabeth was seemingly a dog person, she seemed very interested.

'You'll have to give me the recipe for this millionaire's shortbread,' Maxine said as she bit into a second slice of the homemade confection. 'It's something my customers would love.'

She picked up on Elizabeth's raised eyebrow and instantly worried she might have overstepped the mark.

'Unless it's a family secret, of course,' she rushed to add.

'Angus has the recipe.' Elizabeth glanced over at her son. 'I've a feeling he won't mind sharing. He might even make it for you. He was handy in the kitchen as a boy.'

Angus gave a horrified groan. 'Mum,' he objected. 'Maxine doesn't need to hear any childhood tales.'

'I know about his culinary skills. Angus made me a birthday cake,'

Maxine shared. 'And he made a cake for Teddy, my Selkirk Rex, too.'

Angus squirmed by her side on the sofa, and she almost felt sorry for him as his mother reached across from where she sat in her chair and gave his arm a pat.

'Why don't you take Cindy for a walk,' Elizabeth suggested. 'And let me and Maxine have a proper chat.'

At the mention of the 'w' word, Cindy went bananas. She was just a blur as she barked and yelped and ran towards the door. Angus stared uncertainly after her.

'You can't disappoint her now,' Maxine said.

'With the three of you ganging up on me like this, I suppose I have no choice.' Giving a resigned shrug, he got to his feet. 'I'll be back,' he said as he followed the dog to the door.

'Soon.'

'No need to rush, Angus,' his mother called after him, her voice raised so she could be heard above Cindy's noisy exit. 'And you don't need to worry

— we're both quite fond of you, so the stories will be kind.'

* * *

'Your mother wasn't what I was expecting,' Maxine confided as they drove off.

After the initial awkwardness had been dispensed with, Elizabeth had turned out — under that frown — to be a vivacious and entertaining hostess. Maxine's head was reeling with amusing tales from Angus's childhood.

'Better or worse?' His gaze was firmly fixed on the road ahead, but spotted a tell-tale twitch of his jaw that revealed her answer mattered very much.

Maxine smiled. 'She's lovely.'

Angus smiled back, obviously relieved. And it was only at that point that Maxine realised he had been every bit as nervous about this meeting as she had been herself.

She didn't know now why she'd been so worried, though. It was easy, she had found, for dog people and cat people to get along when they had something in common. And Elizabeth and Maxine had Angus.

'And I adored Cindy. I can't imagine why I was so worried about meeting her. She's a wee sweetie.'

'Cindy loves you, too.' Angus glanced across quickly and winked. 'Though maybe not as much as I do.'

Maxine let out a breath she hadn't known she'd been holding. As declarations of love went, it maybe wasn't the most romantic. They were in the car, his hands on the steering wheel and his eyes, for the most part, fixed on the road ahead.

She had imagined commanding his entire attention at such a moment. She had thought he would take her in his arms. That they would look deeply into each other's eyes. That there would be kisses.

But despite the unromantic setting, her heart skipped a beat. She knew how difficult it would have been for Angus to express his feelings, and his declaration meant all the more to her for that.

'I love you, too,' she told him, a contented sigh escaping her lips because this seemed the perfect setting, after all.

Kisses could wait until they got home.

12

Reported Missing

'There's something wrong.' Maxine sat up in the passenger seat as the car rounded the corner onto the street where her cat café and Angus's shop were situated.

They'd had a lovely time, but anxiety clawed at her now as she got the feeling that things had gone horribly awry in their absence.

'Why do you think that?' He manoeuvred the car into a parking space at the front of his shop.

'I don't know.' Maxine looked around, frantically trying to see what was out of place; what it was that gave her this uneasy feeling in the pit of her stomach despite the fact she was delighted to be back.

Maybe it was because there was a crowd of cats watching the world go by from the window of the café. One or two would be usual, but the majority of Maxine's feline family watching out at one time was unusual. Or maybe it was of the fact the café should be shut, but the blinds were still open. Or maybe it was the small crowd that had gathered on the green in front of the café.

'Things aren't quite the way they should be.'

Angus sighed. 'The cats have been fine whenever we've left them before. Admittedly, we've not been away for quite as long before, but why should it be any different this time? Sabrina's a good assistant, isn't she? And the cats seem fine.' He nodded towards the window to underline his point.

She knew he was right. She glanced across at the curious cats. All seemed well.

And yet . . .

'Look,' she managed faintly, as she pointed to bring them to Angus's attention. 'Sabrina and Chloe are out there with the people on the green.'

Why would Sabrina and her teenage daughter be out here instead of inside the café, where they should be, with the cats?

Maxine's hands trembled as she fumbled ineffectively with the buckle of her seatbelt.

Without a word, Angus reached across, his fingers brushing against hers as he released the catch in one easy move. 'Let's go see what's happening,' he said.

★　★　★

'Maxine — I'm so sorry.' Sabrina was on the verge of tears, Chloe pale-faced beside her, as Maxine and Angus approached.

'What's wrong? What's happened?' Maxine demanded as she glanced instinctively towards the café.

'Oh, Maxine.' Sabrina gave a sob. 'It's Gladys.'

Maxine felt the blood drain from her face and was glad of the supportive arm Angus put around her shoulders.

Gladys had been missing from the cats watching at the window.

She should have realised that was a bad omen. Gladys was always at the forefront of whatever was going on.

Every scary scenario ran through Maxine's mind at once — all the things that might have happened to Gladys. She knew she would have to ask, but somehow she couldn't.

'What's happened to Gladys?' Angus asked when it became obvious that Maxine wasn't going to.

Sabrina and Chloe exchanged nervous glances.

'That's just it,' Sabrina confessed. 'We just don't know. She's disappeared. Mrs Watkins was in just as we were finishing the last guest session. She was causing a fuss because Angus's shop was closed.'

'What has my shop to do with the café?' Angus's voice was gruff as he asked the question — a sure sign he was stressed.

'Nothing. And I told her that. And

when she'd gone we did the headcount, as we always do, and found Gladys was missing. She must have slipped out with Mrs Watkins.'

'Where have you looked?' Maxine asked, her need to find Gladys bypassing shock and horror and galvanising her into speech.

'Everywhere,' Chloe chipped in. 'In the café, the kitchen and the store cupboards, the shed outside in the garden and the entire garden and surrounding area.'

'We're out here trying to organise a search party,' Sabrina said as the crowd on the green began to disperse. 'They're going to search their houses and gardens and check their outbuildings.'

'I'll have a look over my place.' Angus gave Maxine's shoulder a squeeze before dropping his arm. 'She's been found there before.'

Maxine nodded, grateful for the efforts being made to find her beloved Gladys.

'I'll go and have another look in the

café,' Chloe offered. 'Just in case we missed her hiding place the first time we looked.'

'I'm so sorry, Maxine,' Sabrina said again as Angus and Chloe walked off. 'I can't believe I was so careless. I've always known Gladys was a flight risk.'

Maxine, even though worried beyond words, found herself in the strange position of comforting someone equally terrified of a possible negative outcome.

'You mustn't blame yourself. This could have happened to anyone. It has happened before. You know she's escaped while I was looking after her.'

In the past, Gladys had made her way next door to Angus's. Things had always turned out all right before, and they would this time. She had to believe that.

Her heart lifted when Angus emerged from his shop a few moments later — but then sank again when she realised his arms were empty. He shook his head.

Maxine tried not to think of the

possible outcomes. Of how the streets could be a dangerous place for a cat who wasn't accustomed to being outdoors.

'I'll never forgive myself if anything happens to her,' Sabrina said.

Maxine felt the same way about herself. She'd been off galivanting, having fun with Angus when she had responsibilities here. She should never have gone out for the day.

'I know exactly where she's gone . . . ' Angus cut across Maxine's thoughts and she turned to find him staring up at the roof of the café.

An unrepentant Gladys stared down on proceedings with a mildly superior air, almost as though she realised how much trouble she was causing.

'Thank goodness.' Maxine was nearly dizzy with relief.

But before she could begin to solve the problem of how to get Gladys down, it became obvious that someone else was one step ahead. Sabrina's teenage daughter was making a death-defying move to climb out of the dormer window of Maxine's living room, aiming squarely for the cat.

'Chloe,' Sabrina cried, her hands going to her face in horror.

'Chloe, go back inside,' Maxine called, waving her arms frantically.

But Chloe wasn't moving. Only a short distance from the window, she seemed to be frozen to the spot.

'I can't go back.' Chloe's voice was barely audible. 'I can't move.'

Maxine was aware of Angus and Sabrina dashing for the café door and rushed after them, dodging curious cats as she made for the stairs and took them two at a time.

By the time she arrived in the living room, Angus had persuaded Chloe to inch closer to the window, and Sabrina had grabbed her arm to pull her inside.

Once the girl was inside safe and sound, Sabrina threw her arms around her. 'Don't you ever do that again,' she scolded, hugging Chloe so tightly it was a wonder either of them could breathe. 'What on earth were you thinking? You could have fallen. You could have been killed.'

'I thought I'd be able to reach Gladys,' Chloe sobbed, not quite recovered from her ordeal, it seemed. 'But once I got out there, I couldn't move. Should we phone the fire brigade to come and help?'

'Only as a last resort,' Angus replied, making for the window; and sitting on the windowsill, he popped his head out. 'To be honest, if she got herself up there, there's a chance she can get down again without much bother.'

Maxine's heart was in her mouth as she watched. Was he going to climb out as Chloe had done? She knew that as an electrician he was used to climbing all over buildings, but never normally on the outside.

She went over and held on tight to his arm. If he was going to fall, he would have to take her with him.

'Gladys,' he called, and they heard an answering meow from outside. 'We're home. Now stop being silly and come back inside for your tea.'

The words were softly spoken, just as they always were when he talked to the cats. Maxine thought she liked that about him most of all.

Within seconds, the young black and white Norwegian Forest Cat had tiptoed from her perch and nestled comfortable on Angus's shoulder — her favourite place in the world, it seemed.

A loud cheer was heard from the crowd below, and everyone inside heaved a collective sigh of relief.

Angus carefully manoeuvred inside, cat and all, and soon Gladys was enjoying the fuss everyone was making of her.

'She must have sneaked upstairs at some point,' Maxine deduced. 'Rather than going out with Mrs Watkins, like you thought.

'It's my fault,' Chloe confessed, looking sheepish. 'We were running out of milk in the café, and with the shop being closed, I came to see if you had any in your fridge up here. Gladys must have followed me, and I didn't notice.'

'I'd say it's my fault,' Sabrina disagreed. 'It was me who suggested checking in Maxine's kitchen.'

'And I'm the one who opened the window this morning for some air and forgot to close it before I went out.' Maxine nuzzled her face against the cat as she remained resolutely on Angus's shoulder.

'We could just blame me,' Angus said. 'I was the one who suggested an outing last minute. If I'd given Maxine more notice, she wouldn't have left in such a hurry and she would have had time to close the window. Not to mention if I'd been in the shop, you wouldn't have had to come to Maxine's flat for milk.'

'So we're all to blame.' Chloe seemed relieved for an opportunity to share the burden of guilt.

Angus grinned. 'Except I don't think any of us should beat ourselves up about it. Gladys is safe and there's no harm done.'

Sabrina and Chloe left shortly after. And once Gladys had been taken down to re-join her brothers and sisters in the café, Angus and Maxine snuggled up with hot chocolates on the café's most comfortable sofa.

His arm came about her shoulder, and she rested her head against him. And had never felt so happy with life.

Only one thing worried her now.

Cats were dotted here and there, some sleeping, some playing, Gladys safely on Maxine's lap — Maxine was almost frightened to let her out of her sight.

'What am I going to do with her?' she asked, not really expecting Angus to know, but needing to voice her concerns. 'How can we stop her getting out again?'

He ruffled the cutest escapologist behind the ear and earned a contented purr.

'She needs adventure,' he said thoughtfully. 'She needs to be able to get out, to explore. I don't think the café's enough for her.'

Panic gripped Maxine. She knew that what Angus was saying made sense, but the thought of allowing Gladys or any of her thirteen cats the freedom to explore outside made her cold with dread.

'The main road . . . ' she began by way of explanation. 'We're too close to it.'

He nodded. 'I know. I was thinking of something that would let Gladys and the others have a bit of fresh air and outside time, but where they wouldn't be able to get into any bother.'

Maxine lifted her head. 'I've no idea what you're talking about.'

'A catio — a fenced-in outside space so cats can play safely outside.'

'Yes, I know what a catio is, but I'm surprised you do.'

'I've been doing some research online.'

'Angus, have you been looking at cats on the internet? Are you turning into a crazy cat man?'

She would have sworn she could see

the faint trace of a blush on his face. 'Maybe.' He grinned — and her heart flipped as it always did when he smiled. 'But it's a good idea. We can ask Ed to build it across the back of the café,' he suggested. 'And we can make it big enough for a table or two, so customers can sit out there in the summer if they want.'

Maxine had to admit she was incredibly impressed. She would never have thought of building a catio at the café in a million years. But now Angus had suggested it, it seemed a natural progression for the business. Good for her cats — but something different for her customers, too.

'Well?' he asked eventually, when she still hadn't spoken.

'I think,' she said, snuggling closer up against him on the sofa, 'that's a brilliant idea.'

240

13

Dilemma

Maxine smiled as she reviewed the computer screen with a careful eye as she always did before the mad rush of another busy day at the cat café began.

'Bookings are up again this week,' she commented, scrolling through the figures.

Gladys, self-appointed queen of the café, leapt onto the counter to see what the fuss was about, and Sabrina, the café's human assistant, looked up from the cat she was brushing.

'You definitely seem to have appealed to the collective consciousness with this place,' Sabrina replied.

Maxine still couldn't believe how well her little business had taken off. Every single day she blessed her good luck for the idea that had allowed her to make

the move from accountancy to profes-
sional cat lady.

'In fact, we're almost too busy,'
Maxine continued thoughtfully. 'I had
to refuse a party of six for this weekend.
We're fully booked over both days
again.'

Even with a smart new catio at the
back of the café, there was never quite
enough room for everyone, it seemed.
And there was no way that Maxine
could see to expand the business.

She lifted the curious Gladys away
from the computer and closed the
screen. 'I'm beginning to think I should
have taken over bigger premises.' She
had considered a number of larger
properties, but in the end had thought
it wise to start small and keep funds for
unforeseen circumstances.

Maybe that had been a mistake. Not
only was the café losing potential custom,
but she hated to disappoint anyone.

'You'd need more cats if you had a
bigger café,' Sabrina pointed out.

Maxine glanced around at the thirteen

café cats. 'Yes. That would be terrible.' She struggled to keep a straight face. 'I can't imagine anything worse than more cats.'

Both lifelong cat fanatics, Maxine and Sabrina lost the struggle to maintain their composure and burst into laughter.

The prospect, if only in theory, of more cats made their smiles even brighter as they opened the café to the waiting queue.

But Maxine wondered how she could accommodate more visitors without compromising the comfort and happiness of her cats. She'd reached, through trial and error, a timetable of sessions that allowed for plenty of rest for her charges. It was all going so well that she didn't want to do anything that would throw that off balance.

She made a mental note to speak to Angus about it later. He'd be around for dinner once her café and his shop next door had closed for the day. And he was always ready with a friendly ear whenever she needed to talk.

Angus was another reason Maxine was happy with her life.

She really didn't know what she'd do without him.

★　★　★

'I've been offered a job.' Angus dropped his bombshell as soon as he arrived, even before they had exchanged hellos.

Maxine's words about the lack of space in the café died on her lips. Suddenly there were more important things to worry about.

'It pays a good salary,' he told her. 'We wouldn't have to worry that the shop isn't making a profit.'

She nodded. It wasn't a secret that the small grocer's shop next door was in financial difficulty. Though for a struggling businessman who had been offered a lifeline, he looked thoroughly miserable.

'What is this job, Angus?'

'It would be going back to where I began,' he continued. 'To the company where I did my apprenticeship. Near Mum's.'

Maxine knees gave way and she sank onto a handy sofa.

'But that's more than a hundred miles away.'

Immediately she tried to imagine a life without Angus — one where he not only didn't work next door, but where he had also moved away from the flat above the shop. The one right next to her own.

It was not a vision she relished.

He sat down beside her. 'I know.'

Seeming to sense she was in shock, her little cat Sadie leapt onto her lap. Absently, she stroked Sadie's soft fur.

'Mew,' Sadie offered helpfully, and Maxine managed to smile as she cuddled the young cat closer.

'What did you tell them?'

His serious expression made her fear the worst. To think that this morning her biggest problem had been that she needed to find a way to accommodate more customers in her café. That paled into insignificance now she might lose Angus.

'I haven't told them anything yet.' He sighed as he was besieged by Gladys jumping onto his shoulder and Teddy arriving on his knee. 'I wanted to talk to you before I gave them an answer.'

She wanted to tell him not to accept. Not to leave her. To stay here with her and the cats and they'd manage somehow. But she knew she couldn't do that.

'It's your future, Angus. It's not right for me to tell you what to do. It has to be your decision.'

He raised an eyebrow. 'I rather thought it was your future, too.'

She sighed. 'OK. I don't want to lose you.'

Careful not to dislodge any of the cats who were still cuddled close, he put an arm around her shoulder and dropped a kiss on the top of her head.

'You're not going to lose me. But we need to decide what's best. You do my accounts, you know the shop's losing money — it will take a miracle to turn things around. We just need to decide if this job's the miracle we need.'

She nodded, her worries soothed a little by the fact Angus was keen they face this dilemma as a couple.

'But if you accept, it will mean a long-distance relationship.' That didn't sound like a miracle to Maxine. 'I'd miss you dreadfully.'

'I'd miss you, too.' He was quiet for a moment. 'Or . . . ' he began.

'Or what?'

'Or you could come with me.'

She would prefer that option to letting him leave without her. But it would mean leaving her café and taking the cats to start a new life far away.

With a sigh, she lifted Sadie from her knee and put the cat onto the sofa cushion. 'Dinner will be ready by now,' she said, holding her hand out to Angus. 'Let's go and eat and we can think about what to do. You don't have to give them an answer straight away, do you?'

He shook his head. 'I have until the end of the week.'

'Good. Then we can try to put this aside for now and enjoy our meal.'

They had plenty of time to decide.

* * *

Another day at the café, and Maxine made her way downstairs to serve breakfast to her thirteen cats — all of whom were becoming increasingly vocal about their state of hunger.

'OK, my darlings,' she said, picking a careful path through the furry bodies that were vying for her attention. 'No need to make such a fuss. I'm only two minutes later than normal. My alarm didn't quite go off on time.' She smiled at her own joke — her alarm was called Sadie, who slept on the foot of her bed, and made a fuss every morning when it was time to get up.

The cats weren't impressed.

She didn't bother telling them about how badly she'd slept, or how much her head was aching this morning. She knew that all they were interested in was their meal, so she went into the kitchen and began to take out their breakfast dishes from the cupboard to a deafening accompaniment of impatient meows.

Finally silenced by food, her feline family were each and every one too busy eating to even look up when Sabrina arrived.

Maxine turned a bleary eye her assistant's way and raised an eyebrow when she noticed the box in Sabrina's arms.

'What do you have there?'

'It was on your doorstep when I arrived just now. I think you need to sit down before I show you what's inside.' Sabrina put the box onto one of the café tables.

Maxine felt her eyes narrow suspiciously. 'Is someone meowing in there?' Her own cats were silently dining still, so the noise she could hear must coming from the box.

Sabrina nodded. 'There are two of

them.' She opened the box with a flourish, and stepped back so that Maxine could peer in.

Two curious pairs of eyes stared back.

'Oh.' Maxine was immediately smitten by a peachy-coloured mama cat, and her very own mini-me.

'There's a note.' Sabrina pointed to an envelope taped to the inside of the box.

Not wanting to startle either of the little visitors, Maxine placed a cautious hand inside the box. The cat and her kitten weren't in the least concerned as she gently detached the envelope, then tore it open.

'Mum's called Maisie,' Maxine said, scanning the note, headache forgotten. 'And the kitten is Milly.' Maxine smiled at the two residents of the box. 'Their owner can't manage them any longer — they're wondering if I would find homes for them. It's unsigned.' Maxine sighed. 'How could anyone just abandon these two?'

Maxine could feel tears welling at the thought, and she lifted Gladys and Sadie, who had now finished their breakfast and come to investigate, down from the table.

'At least they left them with you,' Sabrina pointed out. 'They know you'll take care of them.'

Maxine nodded. That their owner had been so considerate, at least, was something.

★　★　★

'The vet gave both mum and baby a clean bill of health,' Maxine told Angus later that night as they sat together on the sofa in her flat. 'But she suggested I keep them up here in the flat, out of the way of the others, for now. Only Sadie and Gladys ever come up here, so they'll have some peace and quiet.'

Maisie had climbed onto Maxine's lap and was fast asleep, while Milly played with the laces of Angus's boots. The two had settled in already, and had even made friends with Gladys, who had followed them up from the café.

He nodded, shifting to adjust to Gladys into a more comfortable position on his shoulder.

'And, long-term? What will you do with them?'

Maxine sighed. 'Do as the note suggested, I suppose, and find good homes for them. I'd prefer it if they could stay together.'

'But you want to keep them?'

'Of course I want to keep them.' The words tore from her. 'But that's impossible.'

'Why?'

'Well, the lack of space . . . ' she began. 'The café was planned for twelve, and I'm already accommodating thirteen. And it was only yesterday you suggested I move away with you — it wouldn't be fair to take on more cats until we know what you're going to do about the job.'

'I'm not taking it,' he said. 'My life's here now. With you. And with these

252

crazy cats.' With a gentle touch, he reached up to ruffle the fur under Glady's chin and earned himself an adoring purr.

'But your shop . . . '

'Will have to close.' He sighed. 'There's really no point in keeping it going. That's the one thing this job offer has made me face. I'm a trained electrician — it's daft to be struggling to make ends meet selling the odd pint of milk or loaf of bread to customers who have done their main shopping in the out-of-town supermarket.'

She nodded. 'So what will you do?'

'I could set up on my own.'

She nodded again, liking this version of events more than the one where he accepted the job that was so far away.

'So I have a proposal for you . . . '

A proposal? She felt her eyes widen as her heart began to thump in her chest. 'Yes?'

'Why don't we knock down the wall between the shop and the café so you can expand your business?'

Not the proposal she'd been expecting.

'Then you could keep Maisie and Milly. And maybe get a few more cats besides, if you wanted.'

She definitely wanted. But something was bothering her . . .

'You could sell your place. You'll need the money if you're going to be setting up a new business.'

'The money would be handy, but doing this for you would make me happy.'

She smiled, immediately imagining a café that was twice the size of her existing one. Angus had stepped up to solve her problem, as he always did.

'OK,' she agreed. 'On condition that you let me invest in your new venture. And let me pay for the alterations.'

He quirked an eyebrow.

'I have savings,' she confessed.

He shook his head and smiled. 'Once an accountant . . . '

' . . . always an accountant,' she finished with a laugh.

It made so much sense, and yet . . . She couldn't quite get over her disappointment. For just a moment there, she'd been convinced he was about to make a proposal of an entirely different kind.

He put his arm around her, and she snuggled closer — even if Gladys stopped her quite resting her head on his shoulder.

'And, while we're making alterations,' he continued, 'if we knocked through the flats upstairs, too, they'd make one cosy home for a newly married couple.'

Her head snapped up. 'Angus — are you making me an offer of marriage?'

'What would you say if I was?'

'Yes.' She gave her answer without hesitation, maintaining eye contact as he gave a lazy grin. 'If you were making me an offer then I would say yes.'

'Then I'm making you an offer.'

Without hesitation, but carefully so as not to disturb the cats, Maxine leaned forward and sealed the deal by kissing her new fiancé.

We do hope that you have enjoyed reading this large print book.

Did you know that all of our titles are available for purchase?

We publish a wide range of high quality large print books including:
Romances, Mysteries, Classics
General Fiction
Non Fiction and Westerns

Special interest titles available in large print are:
The Little Oxford Dictionary
Music Book, Song Book
Hymn Book, Service Book

Also available from us courtesy of Oxford University Press:
Young Readers' Dictionary
(large print edition)
Young Readers' Thesaurus
(large print edition)

For further information or a free brochure, please contact us at:
Ulverscroft Large Print Books Ltd.,
The Green, Bradgate Road, Anstey,
Leicester, LE7 7FU, England.
Tel: (00 44) **0116 236 4325**
Fax: (00 44) **0116 234 0205**

Newly widowed Emily believes she will never love again. Working as an assistant in flirtatious Cameron's antiques shop, she finds a romantic keepsake in an old writing desk. Emily and Cameron set off on a hunt for the original owner, and the discoveries they make on the way change both of them forever. But Emily doesn't realise that Cameron is slowly falling in love with her. Is his love doomed to be unrequited, or will Emily see what's right in front of her — before it's too late?

PARADISE FOUND

Sarah Purdue

Carrie's first visit to Chatterham House, where her grandparents lived and worked, becomes an unexpected turning point in her life when her relationship with her boyfriend ends disastrously there; but she meets Edward, a handsome employee who shares her interest in the estate's history. When she begins volunteering at the house on weekends, she feels drawn to Edward — but the icily beautiful Portia seems to have a claim on him, and his only explanation is that it's 'complicated'. Will Carrie decide he's worth risking her heart for?